The Shooter Mystery Short Stories Series

by

gay toltl kinman

Editing & Proofreading by William R. Kinman
Cover designed by Peggie Chan
Photo of gay toltl kinman by Brian and Lilly Loo Studios
Interfacing with Kindle and Amazon by Peggie Chan

Published in the United States of America
By Mysterious Women

Also by gay toltl kinman

MYSTERY NOVELS

Greenway - Four Mystery Short Stories Set on Greenway, Agatha Christie's
Holiday Home in Devon
Death in San Antonio Mystery Stories: Four mystery short stories set in San
Antonio featuring P.I. Brooke
Jo Peters Mysteries: Cases as Assistant District Attorney,
City Attorney & P.I.
Tony Reynolds, CIA Agent: Cozy Thriller Stories
Vengeance Is Mine: Nine cases that are based on real cases—but with a twist
A Man Of Honor: A Marlowe and LAPD Officer Agnes Graham Mystery
Stand Down, Mystery Stories
Death in Hollywood 1942: The Marlowe & LAPD Officer Agnes Graham Series
Death in...17 Mysteries
Death in Hamburg
Murder and Mayhem at The Huntington Library
Wolf Castle (originally published as Castle Reiner)
Death in Rancho Las Amigas
Upclose and Personal
Death in Covent Garden
Death in A Small Town

CHILDREN'S MYSTERIES

The Adventures of Lauren Macphearson
Lauren Macphearson and The Scottish Adventure
Lauren Macphearson and The Colorado Adventure
Lauren Macphearson and The Jumbled Cupboard Adventure
Lauren Macphearson and The Ghostly Adventure

Super Sleuth: Five Alison Leigh Powers Mysteries
The Mystery of The Missing Arabian
The Mystery of The Missing Miniature Books
The Mystery of The Octagon House
The Secret of The Equestrian Park
The Secret of The Strange Staircase

Gilly's Divorce or Don't Make The Mistakes I Did
The Mystery at The Stables

NON-FICTION

Desserticide II: AKA Just Desserts and Deathly Advice
Gilly's Manual and Advice on Coping with Your Divorce
Hidden Heroines of The Huntington

PLAYS

The Play's The Thing: A Collection of Plays
A Little Theater Mystery
Death In Russia
Putting Mother's Seat Belt On
Revenge
The Audition
The Mystery Writer
The Thief
Wicked Well
The Purloined Letter
Not One More Word
The Ashes of Zane Grey
Baskets to Jade
Esther Howland: Queen Of Hearts
(A Ten-Minute Biographical Play)
Esther Howland: Queen Of Hearts
(A One-Act Biographical Play)
Nicholas Owen: Builder Of Secret Places
(A Ten-Minute Biographical Play)
Nicholas Owen: Finder Of Secret Places
(A One-Act Biographical Play)
Home Sweet Murder
Mr. Marshall's Doppelganger
The Deposition
Unscheduled Changeover in Hamburg 1974

AUDIOBOOKS

Death in a Small Town
Death in Rancho Las Amigas

The Shooter Mystery Short Stories Series

A shooting at the airport leaves some dead, including the shooter, and leaves Sylvia traumatized and her husband dead. She has no memory of her life, even her home is not familiar when she is allowed to return. Dr. Rose, her psychiatrist, leads her to a startling revelation.

The second in *The Shooter* series features Celeste, who is affected by the shooting at the airport—how her life has changed radically. She assumes another person's identity—sometimes for the good, and sometimes not.

Sonja is at LAX when a shooting occurs triggering her memory of her last visit to Lido. She recalls the meeting of her upstairs neighbors, and what happened that summer. Sonja recalls all of this as she waits at LAX for a flight that may, or may not, take her back to Lido for her annual summer vacation.

Sybil arrives at LAX, but gets lost in the construction and stumbles into the Departures area where she sees a man who shoots several people. She runs and hopes no one finds out she was there and was a witness.

A shooting at LAX has affected the lives of several women. This is one of the stories. Trudy's suitcase was tampered with—which involved her in the shooter's actions. And through this and the other stories we learn more about the shooter.

Simone and her sister are both injured when the shooter randomly sprays the area with bullets. A life changing experience in more ways than one.

Liana, a shooting victim, has a new face and wants a new life. She wants to have *joie de vivre*—to feel exuberance enough to want to dance in the rain. She learns more about the shooter and wonders what his life was like and why he had to shoot his parents and others at LAX. She feels sad that he, obviously, never experienced a desire to dance in the rain—but he has given her a chance to do that.

To
Dr. Meredith F. Taylor
and
Dr. Susan A. Rowland
with many thanks.

THE SHOOTER

A shooting at the airport leaves some dead, including the shooter, and leaves Sylvia traumatized and her husband dead. She has no memory of her life, even her home is not familiar when she is allowed to return. Dr. Rose, her psychiatrist, leads her to a startling revelation.

THE SHOOTER

She came to consciousness from a deep soft black hole, rising gently to the surface. She was lying in a bed, very comfortable. All was not clear for a moment. Everything was white. Daytime.

A window to her left, the blinds partially open, silhouetted a figure. A woman who turned and spoke. "Sylvia?"

She had to think about the question. Of course, she had a name. "Yes," Sylvia answered.

The woman came closer. Sylvia squinted at the name tag. Dr. Rose Karchoff. "How do you feel?" she asked.

Sylvia did an inventory, moved her toes and fingers. She felt something at her side like appendicitis. "I'm fine."

"Do you remember what happened?" the woman asked.

Sylvia thought what happened when? She felt like she had been newly created—like Dr. Frankenstein had just assembled her. "I think," Sylvia said, "I think I don't."

The woman—Sylvia now thought of her as Dr. Rose—sat down in the chair facing Sylvia. It had been positioned that way, as though the woman had been sitting in it, watching her. "What do you remember?"

Remember? What did that mean? Everything starts now. What did 'remember' mean? Her mind was now. There was no before. "Nothing," Sylvia answered.

"You were shot at," the woman said.

Instantly the scene was in her mind. She was watching it as a movie. Then the movie stopped when she passed out. "Someone with a gun. Big gun spraying bullets all over. We were going through security at the airport. LAX."

"Who is 'we'?" the woman asked.

Sylvia tried to bring the picture back up. "A man next to me. I know him…we're…we're related." The picture disappeared.

"How are you related?" Dr. Rose leaned forward in the chair, a look of intense interest on her face.

Sylvia searched her mind for a word. Husband. "He was my husband—but…something else but I don't know what." Then the realization hit her. "Is he dead?"

The woman was slow to nod.

"How many were killed?" Sylvia asked.

"Five dead. Twenty wounded. Some seriously. Do you remember anything else?"

Sylvia tried to shake her head, but she couldn't move it. "No."

"You don't feel any pain?"

Sylvia said no. She felt nothing. Dr. Frankenstein hadn't perfected feelings and sensations.

"You'll be fine. We'll get you up, moving around. Some massage, physical therapy. Two more days and you'll be ready to leave." The woman stood.

Leave where? Where was she? She tried to remember. They were about to leave, her husband—Giles—fly somewhere, going through security, take off your shoes, that's what she was bending down to do when she saw the shooter.

She didn't know where she was, where were her purse, passport, money... Trying to puzzle it out, her mind shut down.

She had only that one picture of what happened. Nothing else.

"What about the shooter?" she asked, her voice sounding like it came from someone else, but voicing her thoughts.

Again, a long pause, then Dr. Rose said, "He's dead. By a proverbial hail of bullets."

Another woman came in. She was small, dark hair tied at the back. "My name is Deidre. I'm going to give you a little physical therapy. You haven't moved for four days. We need to exercise your legs." As she lifted the sheet on one side exposing Sylvia's left leg, Dr. Rose said goodbye and left. Deidre bent the leg slightly. "How does that feel?"

Sylvia thought yes she could feel that it was attached but that was all. It didn't feel like it was a part of her body, more like something Dr. Frankenstein had attached. A leg from someone else that was now a part of her, Sylvia. "Fine," she answered.

Deidre massaged her calf gently, then bent the leg at the knee and repeated that a few more times. Sylvia could feel the leg becoming more a part of her. Then Deidre pulled the sheet over her leg, went around to the other side and repeated the performance on her right leg. She worked her arms. Sylvia hadn't taken her arms from under the sheet. Now they were also beginning to feel a part of her, too. She was awakening. "I was out for four days?"

"I was just told to give you a light massage, that you hadn't been up for four days."

"What's wrong with me?"

"You were shot."

At least that's what Sylvia thought she said. "Where?" Sylvia could feel no pain.

"At the airport."

"No, I mean where on me?"

"I'll get your doctor. They can tell you more."

Sylvia knew Deidre knew more but in the hierarchy of the hospital she couldn't tell her. "Thank you, Deidre. The massage was lovely."

Deidre smiled. "I'll be back."

Sylvia tried to move her shoulders, but she felt leaden. She wasn't sure she could move anything without Deidre's or someone's help. She knew she was tethered to the bed with a catheter and an IV. That meant she didn't have to do anything. She was glad about that.

Where has she been shot? She brought the picture back up. It was hard to hold it in place in her mind. Too much of an effort. She fell asleep.

When she opened her eyes again, Dr. Rose was there. "Where was I shot?" Sylvia asked.

"Shot? Who said you were shot?"

"Someone. You?"

"Shocked. You were in shock."

Sylvia thought about that. "Why?"

The woman studied her, slightly surprised. "At what you saw."

"What did I see?"

Dr. Rose sat in the chair—orange leather seat and strip at back, worn varnished arms, blonde wood. She stretched her feet out straight, her hands in the pockets of her white lab coat. "You told me what you saw."

"What kind of a doctor are you?" Sylvia asked. The question was out of her mouth without thinking about it.

The woman sat still, as though weighing her answer, the room heavy with silence. "Psychiatrist," She finally answered.

"Are you analyzing me?"

"No. Just trying to help you remember."

"I only have a snapshot," Sylvia said. She couldn't think of any other way to describe the picture in her mind.

"We can try to pull the threads of that, see what we can come up with."

"I don't remember anything else." Sylvia clamped her teeth shut. What was the use of trying to remember when she only had that one image?

"Then let's work with that," Dr. Rose said. "Describe where it takes place."

"Some large room, like a hangar, high ceiling, arches—it's the security place…I have to take my shoes off." Sylvia took a breath. "That's my last thought, bending over to take off my shoes." Sylvia tried to hold the picture in her mind, but it only flashed on her mental screen for a few seconds, then it was gone. "I have to wait for it to come back again. It fades."

Dr. Rose nodded. "You were found bent over, unconscious. At first they thought you had been shot. Or that maybe you had a heart attack. They couldn't unbend you. Like you were in full rigor—or a mummy from Pompeii. They had to give you a muscle relaxant to be able to straighten you out enough to put you on a gurney, put you in a bed so that you could lie straight. Nobody's ever seen anything like that. It took a while to get you unbent."

Sylvia stared at her. "What is wrong with me?"

"Nothing physical. Shock. Trauma. That's why I'm here. You tell me."

"You mean I can get up and go? Leave?"

"Yes."

"Then why can't I move anything?"

"You're still in shock. That's why I have to find out what put you in that condition. Face it. So you can walk out of here."

"I can walk out of here but where do I go? Where do I live?" Sylvia looked away. She felt herself sinking.

When she woke, Sylvia saw that the doctor had dozed off also. But the woman opened her eyes and they looked at each other for a few moments.

"Who was the shooter?" Sylvia asked.

A delay while Dr. Rose seemed to consider the question. "He was 26. Had been in and out of mental institutions, as well as jail, even as a juvenile. Had a vintage Thompson machine gun he stole from a collector. The collector kept the ammunition separate. Someone the shooter knew what went with the gun. The collector does not know how the gun was stolen, and only discovered it missing when the FBI went to his home."

Something flickered in Sylvia's mind. She tried to grab it, but it dissipated like a firefly. "The gun looked like something Bonnie and Clyde used in that movie about them."

"I'd like to try hypnosis, if you would like to participate."

"I feel nothing. No emotion. No feeling in my body. I can't seem to move anything."

"Do you want to?"

"I don't know. As I said, I don't feel anything."

"Then let's try hypnotism. We can do it now." The doctor began talking in a monotone. Sylvia could actually feel herself slipping into a trance. But she didn't feel like she was there long when the doctor asked her how she felt.

"Did I go under? Were you able to get anything?"

"Yes, you're a good subject. You said you didn't want to move, you didn't want to cope. And then some other things that didn't make any sense. I will have to work it out. In the meantime I think you can try to sit up. I'll help you. Let's see how that goes. You can't get out of bed because you still have the catheter in and the IV attached. Let's just do it slowly to see how you feel sitting up. Hold onto my arm."

Sylvia was able to sit up. It felt like she hadn't ever done that before. Everything felt disjointed and her mental messages to move something were not being responded to. Next, Dr. Rose helped get her swing her legs over the side of the bed, careful to keep the things she was tethered to in place. She felt like her brain was sloshing around, trying to settle into place. She wasn't dizzy, for that she was thankful.

An hour later, the catheter was taken out, and the IV removed. Deidre helped her up, placing Sylvia's hands on the bars of a walker. For her first few steps she felt like a toddler—but she was walking. Deidre was pleased, and very encouraging.

Food was going to come at mealtime, and Deidre was going to come back to help her to the bathroom. "You'll have to learn all over again," she said and left before Sylvia could ask what she meant.

Her next physical therapy session was in a large room with others. She had to walk a length, holding onto the railing on each side of her. She felt like she had swim fins on her feet and was walking on dry land with them. She kept looking down, even though she knew there was nothing else on her feet except bedsocks and paper slippers. But her feet didn't know that. Another Dr. Frankenstein hitch. She tried not to lift her feet so high. She stood up straight, took her hands off the railing and tried to walk ignoring the feeling of the fins. She made it to the end, staggering a bit but not touching anything. She had climbed Mount Everest singlehanded!

Deidre was pleased. With her help, Sylvia walked back to the room without using the walker.

Dr. Rose came around to arrange for her release. How to function was coming back to Sylvia. She wasn't ready to be an Olympic gymnast yet, but she felt like she might be able to accomplish some small miracles.

Dr. Rose said she was not finished with her and wanted to visit her until her memory came back. She rode with Sylvia in the back of a car chauffeured by a man. Sylvia remembered nothing and would not have been able to direct him to her home. Dr. Rose told her that her luggage was at her home, but gave Sylvia her purse. Dr. Rose seemed to know the driver, and the driver knew where Sylvia lived. It was nice having people taking care of her, but she looked forward to being on her own—wherever that was. She just wanted to sit and think.

When they arrived, the driver told them to stay in the car and he would check the house. He came back a few minutes later and said it was okay to go in. Dr. Rose helped her out of the car. Standing was not coming to her easily. The driver stood by and watched, only holding open the car door for them. He nodded to Dr. Rose saying that he was going to take a short walk around the neighborhood and wait for her in the car.

Dr. Rose let her walk on her own but stood close. She suggested that Sylvia sit on the sofa while she, Dr. Rose, made coffee.

When drinking coffee, Dr. Rose asked if she wanted her help in putting things away, unpacking, but Sylvia declined. She didn't feel that Dr. Rose's heart was really in that offer, only that she wanted to help if Sylvia needed it.

"Is this all familiar to you?" Dr. Rose asked.

Sylvia thought about how to answer this. "It's not unfamiliar." She looked around. "I've been here before, but it seems all new to me, like I've been gone for a long time. I don't really remember anything— like where this sofa or those chairs came from."

"That comes with shock, trauma. You seem to have been affected more than most." Dr. Rose waited as though Sylvia might offer more. "You have some papers in your suitcase about a house in Italy that you and your husband were selling. Do you remember anything about that?"

Sylvia finished the rest of her coffee, thinking. She shook her head.

"You will, now that you are back in your own home." They talked for a few minutes about the weather, other innocuous things. Dr. Rose told her there was milk, bread and a few other items in the refrigerator, as she knew Sylvia wouldn't be dashing out to grocery shop. They both laughed. Then Dr. Rose left saying she would be back tomorrow morning.

Suddenly Sylvia felt very tired and wanted to go up to her loft bed and climb in. Instead she stretched out on the sofa. When she was completely prone, a bell rang. Sylvia had to think what it could be. The doorbell. She stood, went to the front door and opened it. A woman stood there holding a large orange cat that immediately jumped out of her arms.

Oscar.

The tom wound itself around Sylvia's ankles, purring. She immediately felt a sense of well-being.

"And here's his dishes. I washed them," the woman said as though she expecting praise for her good deed, and handed Sylvia a brown paper bag. She looked past Sylvia as though she expected to be invited in.

Sylvia had a bad feeling about the woman.

"I saw you came home. You're early. Is something wrong?"

"Sick," Sylvia replied, the word out of her mouth without even thinking of an excuse.

"Is there anything I can do for you, make you something to eat? I'll take care of you." She took a step forward.

Sylvia felt revulsed, shook her head and immediately felt dizzy. "Contagious," she said, again without thinking the word, and began to shut the door. The woman stepped back looking doubtful. Sylvia shut the door.

Oscar had already curled himself at one end of the sofa. Sylvia laid down again, her feet on Oscar's warm furry body. She realized she knew the cat's name. That was her last thought.

She was awakened to loud mews, yowlings really, and paper crumpling. Oscar trod on his dishes in the bag. She reached out a hand for him but he was elusive. Petting wasn't on his agenda. What was she to do now?

Sylvia looked up. The room was two stories high with windows around the top. It was getting dark out. The windows around the lower half had wine-colored heavy drapes covering them. She pondered the contrast for a moment, but Oscar was having none of her lollygagging. She stood up and went to the kitchen.

She opened the freezer. On the door shelf was a package that she knew contained cooked chicken,—leftovers from a lunch with friends. She could picture the restaurant, one of the friends, but the other was shadowy. She unwrapped the chicken, put it in a saucepan with a little water and turned the burner to simmer. She went back to get Oscar's dishes, filled one with water and set the other on the counter. In the freezer she found a package of something that looked okay, read the directions and put it in the microwave. She wasn't hungry, but felt anxious, and knew that was a sign that she needed to eat something. She felt like she was moving in slow motion.

Oscar was trying to hurry the process by encircling her ankles, mewing and purring alternately.

After eating, she sat for a long time in the kitchen with just the counter light on. The oval table was encircled on three sides with a padded banquette. The kitchen ceiling was all glass, as was the wall that followed the contour of the banquette. Tree branches surrounded the room, moving slightly in the breeze. The sky was dark now. She could see the street lights and the lights from neighboring houses. No memory came to her, but she liked the place and would have chosen it if she was looking for a place to live. She decided to shower and go to bed, follow what her body was telling her to do.

Leaf-filtered sunlight came in from the top windows, but no rays touched her as both sides of her loft bedroom had walls—one of a closet and the other of a bathroom. She lay there for a moment, then heard

Oscar's yowling. Part Siamese, he had to be with that voice and the long hair. She went downstairs. He sat by the backdoor, yowling. She looked at him. He wasn't asking for breakfast, or he'd be checking out her ankles and staying by his dish. Then she saw the cat door—it was locked. She quickly slid the bolt and off he went. She stood there for a moment looking at the backyard.

A bell sounded. Still slightly disoriented, it took her a moment to realize it was the telephone, the landline, an extension in the kitchen—Dr. Rose asking if it was convenient to come in an hour. Sure.

Sylvia got ready—looking in the closet, trying to assemble an outfit. She realized she could have just opened her suitcase and taken something out. The closet had drawers with underwear and socks. She didn't have time to do a thorough inspection. Showered and dressed, she went downstairs to make coffee as the doorbell rang. Dr. Rose.

Oscar appeared to inspect the guest. Feeling no threat, he curled up at his end of the sofa and did what he did best—nap. A pile of ginger fur so fluffy he looked like a pillow.

With mug in hand, Dr. Rose asked her how she was. "Adapting," Sylvia answered.

"I brought your phone. The driver found it in the car. It must have fallen out of your purse."

A frisson of something went through Sylvia. Dr. Rose was not looking at her as she set the phone on the coffee table, kept her eyes down. A thought skittered through her mind, not stopping to be analyzed. "The driver yesterday?"

Dr. Rose looked at her this time. "Yes."

Sylvia thought about him walking through her house, checking it out, he had said. Why? Before she could consider that more, Dr. Rose said, "Scroll through the directory, see if you recognize any names."

She went through each one. "They feel familiar, but I couldn't tell you who they were or anything about them." She set the phone back on the coffee table.

"What about text or voice mail?"

Sylvia picked the phone up again and checked. She looked at the text ones twice, and listened twice to the voice ones. "Nothing is familiar," she finally said.

"What about your email? Did you check your computer, your laptop?"

Sylvia looked around. Her office. "My office. I haven't been in there—"

"Then, let's look." Dr. Rose stood up encouraging her to move also. She waited for Sylvia to determine where her office was. It took Sylvia a moment and then she went through the door that was under the stairs going up to her loft.

The drapes in her office were open to a view of the backyard, sunny and green. Her desk was to the right. She opened the laptop, pressed the 'on' button and waited for it to come to life. She smelled a faint aroma of aftershave. Not the kind the driver had, not even close. His had not been strong at all. She thought about Giles, her husband—what kind of aftershave did he use? But she couldn't remember. She went to emails and scrolled through them slowly, feeling Dr. Rose watching over her shoulder. "Nothing means anything," Sylvia said. She heard Dr. Rose give a slight sigh, one of disappointment—something like that.

They went back to the living room, Sylvia filling their mugs with more coffee. They were silent for a few moments. Sylvia sat on the sofa, Dr. Rose took a chair opposite. Not hard for Sylvia to be silent as she had nothing to say. Then Dr. Rose said, "Have you thought about your son?"

Sylvia was startled. "I have a son?" Then she thought, "Was he with us? Was he killed, too?" Oscar crawled onto her lap, a puddle of warm fur. She stroked him, feeling comfort from his nearness. He was kneading her leg, purring.

Dr. Rose sighed. It came up from her rope and canvas sandals, past her cocoa colored long silk pants, past her cream silk blouse and brown silk vee-neck pullover, and out of her light-pink painted lips. "He lived in Italy. You were going there."

Sylvia noted Dr. Rose had used the past tense. A feeling of iciness started with her toes, mirroring Dr. Rose's sigh path, crawled up her legs, her chest, and soon she was shivering. Dr. Rose put the sofa's throw around her shoulders and went to the closet by the front door, pulled out a coat and covered Sylvia's legs, slipping part of it under Oscar so that he weighed it down and it stayed in place. She then hurried to the kitchen and came back a few moments later and wrapped Sylvia's hands around a mug. "Just hot water. To warm your hands. Talk to me. I don't want you to go into shock again. What are you thinking?"

"Nothing." The word came out in several syllables because Sylvia's teeth were chattering. Dr. Rose sat beside her, her arm around Sylvia's shoulders, holding the throw in place and tighter.

"Tell me about Oscar," Dr. Rose asked. "He seems to be quite the pet."

"Don't know," Sylvia said, her teeth still chattering.

"Warm up, Sylvia, please. You're going to go into shock again. Sip a little of the hot water." Sylvia's hands were shaking, she could hardly get the cup to her lips, but Dr. Rose helped. Then Dr. Rose started talking—about the flowers in front of Sylvia's house, about food, and slowly Sylvia felt the cold ebbing away, just as it had come—a glacier melting. Dr. Rose encouraged her to lie down, covered her with the throw and the coat. Oscar draped himself over her ankles and Sylvia slept.

When she woke, Dr. Rose had gone and Oscar was making hungry noises again. Sylvia couldn't tell what time it was by the light. Maybe mid-afternoon. She wasn't interested enough to find a clock, or check her phone for the time. She just wanted to float. But Oscar wasn't having that. She got up and found a can of cat food and dry food for him. She had a glass of milk. She knew she should eat. A piece of cheese and a piece of bread. She stood in the center of the kitchen, just staring at the glass almost all around her. She revived a bit then went to her office and looked at each of her emails, slowly and carefully, trying to squeeze out a memory. Nothing seemed to require an intelligent answer, or any answer. If she had planned to be away for a while no one would be expecting anything. At least, that was her reasoning.

Lionel. The name came to her, but she didn't know what it meant. Her mind was just floating. She found it hard to concentrate on anything. Thinking was an effort. She moved around the office, looking at the papers on the desk, the file cabinets, the shelving on the other side of the room that held books, art objects, mementoes from other countries. Her travels? Gifts? None of it meant anything to her, no memories, no remembering—it was all familiar, but she couldn't tell a story about where any of it came from. It definitely was a working office, the books helter-skelter in some sort of arrangement that she couldn't discern at the moment.

She decided to unpack her suitcase, busy herself with where things went, what cupboards and closets held what. She felt like she was snooping into someone's else's life, yet somehow everything seemed familiar. But that's where it ended, she had no memory of anything.

In the morning while she was drinking coffee, the landline rang again. Sylvia thought about her cellphone, still on the coffee table, still on and perhaps dead. She answered the phone. Dr. Rose asking if she could come by, and said she was bringing a colleague. She paused before saying the word, almost choking on it. Sylvia wondered what that meant, but knew she'd soon find out.

They were at her front door in minutes. They sat in chairs facing Sylvia, who sat on the sofa. Oscar had disappeared. Dr. Rose was not her usual calm self. She sensed this from the way Dr. Rose fidgeted, glancing at the man while talking to Sylvia of inconsequential things. What she said didn't penetrate her brain because Sylvia was absorbed in watching the man who sat as though he was on a throne. He looked around, surveying—with distain—his surroundings, as though he was in a mud hut in the middle of—

"The situation is this, Mrs.—" Missus the word was strung out—"Fairfax," he said over Dr. Rose's words. We do not believe you have lost your memory."

The royal We came across loud and clear.

"We believe you are obstructing justice, hampering this investigation because of your involvement."

Sylvia analyzed his words, knowing what he was saying, but not understanding why he was involving her.

"Obstructing justice is a federal crime for which you will be tried, convicted and imprisoned."

Dr. Rose gasped. "Mr. Carleton! You promised. We agreed—"

But he talked over her again, ignoring her as an underling female, a gnat to his elephant magnificence. He went on with such venom that Sylvia saw his face turn into that of a jackal, spewing spittle as he ranted. Sylvia hardly heard his words but recognized his anger, and knew he was impotent, clutching at a leaky life ring to save himself. Desperation was in his voice. Sylvia just studied him, and realized it was the author in her who was sitting there watching him. She knew she was a writer. The knowledge came to her in a flash. Always taking notes. She wanted her pad and pen, a laptop, something to write with and on.

"We believe you knew all about the shooting, the attack, and that you are withholding crucial information."

Sylvia looked down and noticed the white tiles of the floor, iridescent, almost glazed with a pearly substance, and at her feet a blood red rug. Blood. The floor and the rug rose to her face.

When she came to, the man was gone, but Dr. Rose was still sitting in her chair, watching Sylvia who was lying on the sofa covered with the throw and a coat, Oscar warming her ankles and feet. "What happened?"

"You fainted. At least that's all I hoped it was. I threatened him with calling the paramedics, rushing you to the hospital with a relapse and threatening to report him for his harassment. He left in a huff." Dr. Rose smiled. Sylvia realized it was the first time she had seen her smile and how beautiful she was.

"Help me up, please."

Dr. Rose rushed to her, moving her feet from under Oscar to the floor, and helping her to sit up. She put on Sylvia's shoes, adjusted the throw around her shoulders. "How do you feel?"

"I feel like I want to write down what happened. I'm a writer?"

"Journals, magazines newspapers, TV, internet. Yes, you're a writer. Do you remember anything else?"

"I don't even remember that. All I know is that I want to write. But first, why does he think I'm involved? I didn't understand what he was talking about."

Dr. Rose gave another deep sigh, stood up and went back to the chair where she was sitting. "Does the name Lionel Murray Fairfax mean anything to you?"

"Lionel. That's familiar but I don't…can't tell you why. Was he the shooter?"

Dr. Rose sighed again. This time the sound was one of reluctance. "Yes."

"Oh." Sylvia tried to search her memory, she didn't even know what that was anymore. There was a steel door firmly shut when she tried to go down a path. She shook her head and spread her hands in a futile motion.

Dr. Rose watched her for a few minutes, then said, "He was your son."

Sylvia felt the coldness rising from her feet again, she shivered violently. Dr. Rose moved to her side, adjusting the throw around her, massaging her hands. "You're going to be all right. You now know the fact you've been avoiding. Now you know, you can face it. There's no reason to hide it anymore. Your memory is going to come back." She kept talking to Sylvia soothingly.

Oscar appeared and claimed his place on Sylvia's lap. Dr. Rose placed Sylvia's hands on his warm furry back. They sat that way for a long time.

"He was such a difficult child," Sylvia said. "Never properly diagnosed, we felt. Medications worked for a while, then they didn't anymore. They all had side effects which he hated. And so did we. Solved one problem but created another. He'd disappear—that's when he was older—and we'd never know where he was. Then he'd come back. He never carried any I.D. but once in a while we'd get a call from a police department. Somehow they'd find out who he was. Fingerprints I guess. He could be anywhere in the U.S. We bought the place in Italy, on Lido in Venice. We had been there on a vacation, the three of us. It was the only place where he seemed happy, calm. He had a caregiver. We left him there, came back. We relaxed a bit, then we realized we were only staying together because we had a common problem that we had to solve. We had no other reason. I didn't like the house we lived in. Giles had chosen it without my input. I couldn't write there, not that I was home often. I took every traveling assignment I could. I was away a lot. I didn't want to return. So we decided to get a divorce. I bought this place. He didn't like it at all. Lionel came back to live at home—essentially with Giles. They always got along better than Lionel did with me. A man thing I guess."

Sylvia got up, moving Oscar, the throw, the coat, and went to a shelf across the room. Below the closed drapes was a line of built-in bookcases. She came back to the sofa and sat down where she had been. She opened an album and began showing Dr. Rose pictures of Lionel as a child and through the years, telling her about events, the ones where Lionel was happy, and they were a normal family.

"Since Lionel had come back, we decided to sell the house on Lido. That's what the trip was about. We were going to Italy. I also got some assignments writing about the Biennale, how to sell a house in Italy." Sylvia shrugged, "It's what I do. I write about everything in my life."

"You've done well, Sylvia. Remembering. It's not your fault. You did the best you could under the circumstances. There are no guarantees that we will all have perfect children." Dr. Rose said more comforting things.

Sylvia felt at peace now. The trauma was over. The worst had happened. Now she had to cope with the future. The future with all her memories. "Would you…would you open the drapes?" Sylvia asked. "Drawstrings are on the left side." Dr. Rose did as asked, pulling them all to the side of the great room's lower windows.

Light. Outside was greenery, trees, bushes and window boxes of red and pink geraniums. Sylvia pictured at the back, outside of her office, the brick wall covered with different shades of bougainvillea. Light and color, that's what she liked.

The light filtered through the tree branches and patches of sun wavered as the leaves moved in the light breeze.

The oppressive dark air of the room lightened. Now it looked like the side and front walls were all glass, and on her right the kitchen with its all glass ceiling and end wall.

She felt lighter, too. Lionel was no longer suffering, pulling her down into depression because she was so connected to him, no longer anchored by him. Poor Lionel, he had suffered so much, never feeling a moment's happiness. He didn't know what happiness was. Was his pain so bad that he had to kill other people along with his parents?

Dr. Rose had needed to facilitate her memory restoration and she did that. But Sylvia was sure the care Dr. Rose gave her was to help the FBI, that she was not an employee of the hospital. The Jackal would still think she, Sylvia, knew more than she said. He would be telling everyone he had shook loose the tree—forced her to remember. He would take the credit for bringing back her memory, shocking her into the present with his methods. Maybe he had. Maybe Dr. Rose wouldn't have said anything if she, Sylvia, hadn't asked what the Jackal's visit was all about.

Dr. Rose came back to her after opening the drapes and touched her hand. "You're warming up. Is there anything I can do for you?" Sylvia shook her head. "Then I will leave you alone. You have my number."

Sylvia could only nod in response, and watched Dr. Rose leave. She leaned her head back on the sofa, suddenly it had become too heavy to hold up.

She must have dozed off because Oscar was moving around, trying to wake her. Meowing. His Siamese part yowling. It was getting dark outside. Dinnertime for him.

She heated some soup for herself and fed Oscar, filled his water bowl. Really he had to go on a diet. She realized she had had that thought before.

She left the drapes open. She would change into pjs in the bathroom, not turning the light on in her bedroom.

Giles hadn't liked the house when she bought it, but she loved it. He kept their old place, comfy there, but she had to move, get out, make a place of her own. The house had been owned by a writer and that made it all the more appealing to her. The ghosts of muses hung around for sure. She could only dream about that.

She thought about Lionel. Her presence had seemed to agitate him more, so she had not gone to see him when he moved back into the old homestead. She would only see him if he asked. He was unpredictable, so he might or might not ask to see her.

But that was all in the past. She had cared too much, always fussing about this or that Giles had said—often. He had seemed more relaxed, maybe that's why Lionel had wanted to live with him, related to him more.

She went into her office, sat at the laptop and started to write.

THE SHOOTER

By Sylvia Fairfax

She felt at times that giant meat hooks were embedded in her shoulders and from them were giant chains wrapped around grey boulders of a hundred pounds each and she was dragging them wherever she went. Sometimes there was also a hook in her stomach with another boulder attached.

~The End~

THE AIRPORT

The second in "The Shooter" series features Celeste who is affected by the shooting at the airport—how her life has changed radically. She assumes another person's identity—sometimes for the good, and sometimes not.

THE AIRPORT

Celeste crouched on the floor at the airport. The first sounds had been a rat-a-tat-tat like firecrackers exploding in succession. The sounds with a fraction of a second between. Several. At the first sound—instinctively—everyone dropped—as did she. The woman beside her fell a few seconds later. Then different sounds of gunshots. No sound for a few seconds.

Shouting!

The woman next to her lay sprawled face down on the floor, unmoving. The handle of Celeste's suitcase was under the woman and her outstretched hand offered Celeste her passport. That's how Celeste saw it, her mind numb. She reached forward and took the woman's passport. Then she slid her own purse toward the woman, and pulled the non-descript person to her. An exchange. She quickly looked inside the passport. *Edna Brown*. Their descriptions matched more or less.

She heard running footsteps. She closed her eyes and slumped forward. She heard footsteps and then "We've got two more here," a man yelled.

Then she felt his hand on her wrist. Celeste opened her eyes and looked at him. He was wearing dark blue coveralls with a badge and lettering that she couldn't read.

"Are you all right, ma'am?" he said to Celeste.

Her mouth was glued shut and she couldn't get enough air in to breathe. She could only nod. The man touched the prone woman and Celeste saw that the back of the woman's brown blouse was darker. Wet. Blood.

Something hot rose in Celeste's throat and she gagged, then she heard herself moan.

The man stood, shook his head and clicked on his phone.

"Are you injured? He asked.

"No. Shaky."

"Yeah…well…I can sure understand that." He paused, studying

the prone woman. "I'll get you a wheelchair. We need to move you out of this area."

Fine with her. The floor was cold and there was a draft. The area was open, more like a loft with arctic air rushing up the staircase and the escalator from the open area below. The terminal at this point was about three stories high. She realized she was also shaking from the cold.

He moved away, talking into his phone.

Moments later an attendant with a wheelchair soon appeared and helped her onto it. "Is that your bag?" he asked. He pointed to a carry-on with a pink wool tie that sat at the end on the counter next to the prone woman. Her own suitcase was still partially under the dead woman.

"Yes," Celeste croaked.

The attendant put it in a metal bin at the back of the wheelchair and pushed Celeste to a large room where others were, everyone looking disoriented. Officials in uniforms or with letters on their jackets moved around, talking to everyone. Celeste realized they were taking statements. Others offered fruit juice, hot drinks, cookies.

Celeste took a glass of pineapple juice and drank it in one gulp. Then, from another tray, a mug of hot chocolate. She held her hands around the mug, trying to warm them. The room they were all in was a little warmer. At least no cold draft. A nurse, Celeste read from the name badge, asked her how she was. Celeste said, "Just shaky." "No injuries?" the nurse asked. "No, nothing." "You're lucky," the nurse said. Celeste wondered about that. Was she lucky? Was being alive lucky? Being un-injured definitely was. She drank the hot chocolate quickly, willing it to warm her insides. Then she traded the empty one for a full hot one when someone with a tray came around. Finally she felt a little warmer, but she was still shaking. She had to stop that. It was too annoying. She knew she was in shock, but she didn't want to be. She took a large chocolate chip cookie from an offered tray, then was handed a sandwich. She only want-ed the cookie, but she wasn't strong enough to refuse the offered plastic container of a sandwich cut in half to show its contents. Her stomach revolted at the look of it. She ate the cookie, nibbling on it, savoring the melting of the chocolate chips in her mouth. Nothing had ever tasted so good. The clear plastic box container with the sandwich slid off her lap. A man picked it up and tried to give it back to her.

"You keep it," she said. He took it without comment. Pulling off the plastic, he took out a half. He ate it as fast as Celeste had drunk the first mug of coffee. Then he ate the second half, almost as though he didn't know what he was doing. Perhaps he didn't. He seemed in a trance. *No different from me*, Celeste thought, trying not to watch him. His mouth opened as he chewed. She concentrated on the cookie and tried not to look at him. Thankfully he moved away.

"Are you Edna Brown?" A man in a Marshall's uniform stood in front of her.

She looked around and then at him. He was still looking at her, waiting for an answer. Had someone seen her switch identities? Identities. That was it. That was her new name.

She nodded.

"I'm to escort you to your new home," he said.

A Marshall? Edna had been a prisoner? A witness? What was a Marshall doing here?

Too late now for her to go back. She couldn't.

"Let's go, then," Celeste said. Onward with her new life, but it was looking like it was her old life.

He got behind her and pushed. Then the thought struck her on what the Marshalls do—the Witness Protection Program. Celeste almost laughed out loud, the first real laugh she'd had in years. Maybe things would work out after all.

Celeste thought about the passport she had taken. Was it a fake in that the dead person was not really Edna Brown? It was not a fake because it was probably made by the real Passport Office.

Now the fake Edna had a real passport—Celeste's, and she, Celeste, had a fake one. In any other situation it would have been funny.

What if the Marshall pushing her was fake?

They left by a side door where a van was parked. The Marshall helped her into the van, and took the wheelchair back into the building. He put the carryon, now hers, in the seat behind her.

"Someone will get your other suitcase," he said, as he started the engine. "Ever been to Los Angeles before?"

Celeste was startled, and about to say, *I live here*. Luckily, her mouth was dry and words did not come out easily. She realized Edna was an 'Arrival,' not a 'Departure.' "Mmmm." She almost hummed it in answer. Suddenly she had an insight. If Edna had been in L.A. before, the Marshalls Service never would have sent her there. She had to go to a place where she had never been, didn't know anyone. *Was he testing her?* She wanted to ask about the shooting but didn't.

"We're off to Pasadena, real nice place," he said.

Did he mean Pasadena was a real nice place, or where she was going to be staying? It didn't matter. Suddenly she was so tired, she leaned her head back and her last thought was that if he wasn't who he said he was then she was drifting into the Big Sleep.

The next thing she knew was the driver had stopped at the curb on Marengo Avenue. She knew exactly where she was. California court architecture of three small bungalows on each side of a narrow walkway that led to a two-story house. Greene and Greene-style. They were brothers who adapted Japanese lines to the California climate. In front of each was a small porch with an overhang held up by white pillars. A wrought-iron gate barred the way to the walkway. An addition not seen in other courts, Celeste knew.

The home for those on the program, she was sure. A home for Celeste—or rather, Edna. Not far from the area and people she was trying to escape from. A little curveball in life. She'd have to make do. Since it wasn't likely she'd have to go out much—at least not at first—she'd be safe here. Wasn't that what she wanted—to be safe? Isn't that why she switched passports? That was a desperate move to become someone else. And now she was. But she was still in the danger zone. How long before someone spotted her?

She couldn't worry about that now. *Live in the present.*

A woman came down the walkway toward them. Sturdy—she had lost her waist long ago—in a cotton dress of faded flowers, pale blonde hair, striding confidently. *The warden?*

The woman unlocked the gate and came to Celeste's side of the van as the driver lowered the window. "Welcome, Edna. You're safe now."

Celeste could only wish that were true. The real Edna, or the one she had exchanged passports with, was certainly safe now. But that wasn't the kind of safe Celeste wanted to be. Celeste only nodded.

The driver got out and met the woman at the back of the van. "I heard about a shooting at the airport. What happened?" the woman asked.

"Don't know the details. Some guy with an automatic something. At least five dead. They brought him down, too."

"Was he after—?" Celeste imagined the woman had indicated her.

"Don't know if he was after anyone—just a berserko. I got her out of there as soon as I could. Her carryon's behind the seat. Someone will bring her other suitcase later."

"Coming in for coffee?" the woman asked him.

"Wish I could. Gotta get back. Thanks."

"Anytime. Coffee's always on."

"Gotcha."

Celeste's door opened. "Come on, let's get you settled in. You've been through enough trauma for a lifetime," the woman said. She reached behind the seat and pulled out the carryon. Celeste awkwardly slid off the seat with her feet on the curb. Then leaning on the doorframe to pull herself erect. She tested her weight on her legs and feet and seemed to be okay. She pushed all of her thoughts of the past to be in the here and now. This was her new life.

The driver was back in his seat. Celeste realized he was waiting for her to close the van's door. She grabbed the purse. "You're in good hands, Miss Brown. Things will get better." He started the engine. Celeste closed the van's door. He drove off.

The woman was holding the gate open for her. "Can you manage okay?" she asked. Celeste nodded. She realized she was walking awkwardly. The woman closed and locked the gate after Celeste made her way through. They went to the house at the end of the walkway. She took Celeste to the second floor and showed her the bedroom in front, the master over the front door. Two smaller bedrooms on each side of the stairs. The house looked like it had been built for a family, bedrooms for the girls and for boys, with mom and dad in the room she now occupied.

"Come down for coffee, or tea, if you prefer and a little something to eat, and we'll talk, get you acclimatized. You're safe now," she said again, as she paused in the doorway, then turned and went down the hall to the stairs.

Celeste felt in a dazed state, everything unreal. She had to consider this a vacation, forget her thoughts and fears. Was she safe? She could arrange to change the color of her hair, different style.

She sat, for a moment, at the desk facing the window on Marengo. The desk, chair, bedside tables were of the Mission style. The lamps, faux Tiffany. She stared out to the street, traffic driving by in a steady pattern. Where were they all going? They were going someplace but she wasn't. What was her future? Definitely better—no matter what—than it had been before she became Edna. She didn't like the name, never would have chosen it, but it was hers now.

Enough! Time for coffee.

She joined Joyce, that was the woman's name, in the U-shaped kitchen. The table was small, wooden, sturdy—about the size of the folding card table her mother used to play bridge on.

Joyce poured coffee into mugs for them and offered milk and sugar but it turned out they both took it black. Both mugs had a little red heart on it that reminded Celeste of Valentine's Day.

"We share the work load around here. Saves money, but also keeps out anyone who's not a resident. None of us want the world to know our business. You okay with that?"

"Sure." Celeste nodded. Besides, what else did she have to do?

"We take turns so no one gets stuck forever with something they hate doing. We rotate with the cooking, but there's some who are better than others, so we rotate a little slower here in the kitchen on certain days." She laughed. Her laugh was in the guffaw range, not musical.

Celeste nodded. At the moment the thought of food roiled her stomach. She couldn't remember when she had eaten a meal last. Didn't try to remember. Seemed unimportant and she didn't want to think about the past. About yesterday. What she wanted was to find out something about Edna's past. Why was she sent here? What should Celeste know about who she was supposed to be?

"You don't have to do anything until tomorrow. Just make your bed in the morning. Straighten up your room, that's all. Breakfast is at 8. Some of the moms feed their kids earlier because they have to go to school."

Celeste took this all in, kids, school. Almost normal. She liked that. She nodded again, a regular bobbing head.

"Anything in particular you'd like to do?"

"What do you mean?" Celeste had no clue how Edna was supposed to answer.

"You like art? Going to museums? We have some lovely ones in the area."

Was this a trick question? Was Joyce supposed to pump her, find out more about Edna's life—or whatever her life was before she was christened Edna by the U.S. Marshalls Service.

"Haven't had much time to spend in any. Yeah, I like museums." Celeste almost held her breath. Was that the right answer?

"Terrific. I'll take you to the Norton Simon tomorrow. Just can't get enough of that place. They have a lily pond that could have been painted by Monet." She smiled. "And The Huntington. Love that place. We'll go there, too, if you want." Joyce looked at her.

Celeste couldn't read her expression. Joyce looked like she was afraid Celeste would refuse. No, that couldn't be it.

"I'd like that," Celeste answered after a pause. That seemed to be the right answer because Joyce smiled again.

"Good. It's settled then. How about a ham and Swiss cheese sandwich?"

The next day, Celeste awoke to the smell of coffee and sunshine at the edges of the shades that didn't quite cover the window. The frothy white curtains couldn't stop the light either. Celeste just lay there wondering what would happen if she never got up.

But she did, washed and dressed, made the bed and went down to meet the other denizens of the complex.

The children ranged in age from a baby in a high chair to four teens. She was introduced all around and listened to their chatter about the day, who was making lunch and what.

A flurry as the two teens left for high school, the younger ones for the school bus and the babies and toddlers to a play room where one of the women looked after them.

No one asked her anything about herself. She realized no one would and she couldn't ask anyone about their life either. In a way, that was good—everything equal, no comparing family status or education or anything else that pegged a person on the social ladder. But it was also a little eerie, like being in the after-life.

The others chatted about the weather, their kids. There were ten women. Someone commented they lived next door and waved to another building. So the complex was more than just the bungalow court. Celeste said little, showed interest in whoever was talking and tried to blend in. She was the new kid on the block. Everyone was someone else, maybe their own personality, but a different name and now a different life. But the sense was they were all in this together, they all needed each other— and in that, they were all equal.

She learned each was good at something. Carly was a great seamstress, Molly a great cook, Bridget could fix anything, particularly the old plumbing of the buildings. "And Lola's good at bookkeeping." A guffaw and a snicker from someone, but the others looked away or busied themselves drinking from their mugs. Was Lola's background known? Or did it have to do with something else?

Just then Joyce came downstairs, into the kitchen. "Anyone want more coffee?" A few 'no's replied. That seemed to be the signal to leave as the women were getting up, taking their dishes to the kitchen. Joyce came to the table and sat by Celeste. One of the women began clearing away salt and pepper, sugar bowl, ketchup. Celeste guessed that was her duty for the day.

"You'll soon learn everyone's name—at least the one they've been assigned," Joyce laughed. "I have a few things to do, so let's plan on taking off at 10."

Celeste nodded.

"Did you eat?"

Celeste shook her head.

"Have something. There's oatmeal left. Betts," she said in a louder voice, "Will you bring some oatmeal for Edna?" Then to Celeste she said, "We usually have oatmeal, toast…If Molly's on duty we have great omelets. We haven't starved yet." Another bark of a laugh.

Betts brought them both bowls of oatmeal, brown sugar and milk. Celeste saw the bowls had little red hearts on them, like the mugs. It was such a nice touch, she felt tears stinging her eyes. There hadn't been many hearts in her recent life.

"Real oatmeal. Steelcut. Made from scratch," Joyce said, as she spooned it up.

Celeste found she could keep it all down and emptied the bowl.

Betts filled their mugs. Joyce talked more about how they all lived. "No TV in this room—our Gathering Room—but the apartments and bungalows can have them if they want. People congregate here after dinner—if they want company. We've got books, someone's always working on a puzzle there." Joyce waved at a small table where a jig-saw puzzle was half-finished. A scene from Venice—the Grand Canal. A painting by Canaletto, Celeste knew.

"I'm a nurse," Joyce said, "so I'm the first line of defense for whatever ails you." She smiled. "How are you doing?"

Celeste wasn't sure if that was a rhetorical question or if she really wanted to know.

"Fine," Celeste finally answered.

"Okay, let me know when you're not." Joyce drank the rest of her coffee, stood and carried her dishes into the kitchen. Celeste realized that clattering had been going on in there. She sat for a minute longer, then followed with her dishes.

She went up to her room. There had been toiletries in the bathroom for washing and moisturizing. She had scrubbed her underwear and socks with the bar of soap last night and was wearing them now. She had found a blouse in the carryon and wore that with her own long pants that she had sponged off. Now she looked through the carryon. A jumble of stuff—as though Edna had grabbed and thrown things in there. A pair of shoes. Amazingly they fit. Edna had been about her size. A wig. Celeste tried it on. A complete change in her appearance. Good. She wondered if she should wear it, and decided she would. That would really make her Edna.

The suitcase had appeared also. Again, jumble of clothes, two books, an empty purse, socks, some underwear, even a hat. Celeste hung up what she could, welcoming the different clothes, the persona of the new Edna, and put away the other items in drawers of a Mission-style dresser with a heavy mirror. She felt around in the lining of the suitcase and carryon. Nothing. Maybe Edna had packed everything carefully but it had been jumbled by some Marshall, or even a TSA person. Or someone searching for something. An eerie thought. What were they looking for?

Celeste went back to her original surmise. Either Edna had packed quickly, or she was not naturally a neat person. At least now Celeste had something to wear, nothing worse than had been in her own suitcase.

Celeste took a breath. She was alive and here, time to make the best of it. Time to meet up with Joyce.

"Oh," Joyce stared at her. "I didn't recognize you at all with that wig." She stood and studied her for another minute longer. "No one will ever recognize you."

Celeste felt relieved. That's all she could ask for at the moment. If only she could get into Edna's persona. She'd have to make it up because Edna had been 'born' when the passport was made. She had no history—no *legend*—before that. What did the person who selected the name think? Did that person have a background in mind? Ah, she shook her head trying to shake off the thought—and then was reminded of the wig on her head as it shifted.

Joyce drove them to the Norton Simon Museum of Art—not far, perhaps two miles. Something Celeste could have walked. Which reminded her that she needed to get into some sort of exercise program.

She loved the brown curved building. She'd been there before but not often. Somehow visiting museums had been a luxury timewise that she couldn't fit in—or explain the time away.

Joyce had a membership so they were able to enter right away. "Let's look in the bookstore first."

Celeste followed—then froze. There he was. He didn't see her. What was he doing in a museum? Casing it? She turned slowly, no abrupt movements to catch his eye, and she went to the ladies room. How long could she stay there? Joyce would be wondering what happened to her. Maybe thinking the worse—that Celeste had run away, escaped the program. She couldn't tell Joyce the truth.

She stood in front of the mirror wondering why she didn't see herself. Then she remembered about the wig and laughed. A woman looked at her and moved away. Celeste gave a quick look in Edna's brown mundane plastic handbag. It was truly dreadful. Not much in it. But more than the Queen had probably.

Celeste peeked out. When she didn't see him, she went to the bookstore. He wasn't there. Joyce was looking a marked-down art books. "You okay?" She asked without looking up.

"A touch of diarrhea, but I'm fine."

"We'll fix you up when we get back. I was worried you saw someone you knew."

Ooooh.

"They wouldn't recognize you," Joyce added, still looking down at the book.

Whew.

Celeste said nothing, looked around a little, trying not to check out everyone who came into the small store.

"Let's walk around then we can have coffee outside."

They strolled through the four galleries on the main floor. They moved slowly not pausing long in front of anything. Celeste had to remember to pretend she hadn't been there before. She knew there was East Indian and Asian art downstairs, and sometimes a special exhibit, but she didn't say anything. That art was what the actress Jennifer Jones liked. She had been married to Norton Simon, and had been his widow. Celeste tried to be nonchalant, not looking around. Joyce was non-descript, so the two of them together shouldn't attract anyone's attention.

Enough time had passed, Celeste hoped, that he was gone. Although it was quite likely he was outside drinking beer.

Her luck held.

"You pick a place by the pond and I'll get coffee," Joyce told her.

Celeste sat down at the water's edge. Two swans and three ducks floated back and forth, possibly looking for food to be tossed to them. The lily pads were in bloom. Yes, it was like Monet's painting of his garden. Celeste had never seen his garden, but she felt she was there now. It offered peace.

Joyce came back with a tray of coffee and a bakery goodie. "This is my favorite place," she said as she set the tray down.

"It's lovely, truly lovely," Celeste said. She felt a peace settle over her like she hadn't known for a long, long time. The pastry was delicious, perfect with the hot, strong black coffee and the wonderful view. As though life couldn't get any better. Celeste held that feeling as long as she could.

Joyce kept looking at the pond, like she felt the same way.

On the way back, Joyce said, "Some of our ladies are domestic violence victims. It works just like Wit-Sec—only those ladies are under another group, a separate program, but the principles are the same. They go where they don't know anyone and have never been before. That's so the abuser can't find them. Same principle as Wit-Sec." Just wanted you to know. We had a guy once—domestic violence case. His wife was beating up on him." She sighed. "Takes all kinds."

Wit-Sec? Witness Security? Celeste was surprised at the information and doubly surprised that Joyce had told her. Some of the conversations she'd heard at the breakfast table now made sense.

"We try to find jobs for everyone, get them settled in the community—wherever in the area they want to go. Send them to classes at PCC—that's Pasadena City College. Can do some online. Most of all we offer stability, particularly for the kids. I was always moving around. My dad was in the Air Force. Different schools, but the same somehow—all the kids were like me, being moved around. Sometimes we ran into each other at another posting. We all thought that was a normal life." She laughed.

Celeste mulled all of Joyce's words over. She wondered if Joyce did this for each new arrival. Mother Joyce. "I want to do my part, so let me know what my duties are."

"You did your duty today by coming with me to the museum. It's my Mental Health Day." She laughed again, a loud chuckle. "Have another M.H. Day coming up. You game for a trip to see art and gardens? The Huntington—I love it there, too."

"Sure. Mental Health Day. I like that."

The next morning she waited until 8 to go down for breakfast. All the kids were gone, the babies and toddlers in the nursery in a room in the house, and the rest of the women sitting around talking until 9, the time breakfast was over and everyone did their assignments or went to work, if they hadn't gone earlier. Celeste didn't say much, but they included her in their conversations. Celeste felt the comradery. Joyce didn't come down until 9. Celeste wondered if she, Joyce, felt that the women wanted to talk among themselves without feeling that Joyce would report everything.

At The Huntington, the long walkway to the grounds was lined with all kinds of foliage, small trees, flowers, cactus, large pots of overflowing branches, all leading to a waterfall-type-fountain that flowed over steps. Celeste found it mesmerizing. A very small lily pond at the bottom. Only a hint of Monet.

"Let's go to the house. It's where they lived, only now it's called the Art Museum." In the main gallery, Joyce told her about some of the paintings. British full-length portraits including *Pinkie* and *Blue Boy*. Joyce spent time gazing at each painting, while Celeste sat on the bench in the middle of the room, slowly pivoting and looking at each portrait in the long gallery.

Joyce floated, pirouetted, side stepped—she was dancing, Celeste realized. She could only watch her mesmerized by her graceful movements. Clearly she was enjoying herself. A different person from the in-charge Joyce at the house.

Then Joyce joined her on the bench. "This is all mine, I own everything—but I'm so generous I let other people see what I have." Joyce giggled. Yes, definitely a different person.

Back at the house she and Joyce were having coffee at the big table when the door opened. A man said, "You said I could come for coffee anytime."

It was the driver.

"Hey, Biff, good to see you. Come sit, I'll get you coffee. Fresh pot, too."

Biff sat, a chair away from her, his forearms on the table, his legs stretched out—his body shaped like a V on its side. He didn't look at Celeste or acknowledge her in any way. What did that mean? That he had bad news for her? Or was he just not a sociable guy?

Joyce came back with a mug for him. "So tell us what the news is about the shooting at the airport. Who was he? Why did he do it?"

Biff glanced at Celeste as though deciding what to say. "They know who it was. They don't know why. They're following up on some leads, they say, and are close-mouthed about it. FBI." He added in case Joyce and Celeste didn't know who 'they' were.

"They might want to interview you again." He looked at Celeste. "You told them when you saw the woman's face, you fainted and hadn't come to until the paramedic was taking your pulse." He was still looking at Celeste as though waiting for an answer. She nodded.

"I'm the contact person in case they want to talk to you again." He shifted his gaze to Joyce. "The guy stole a vintage machine gun, loaded it and shot away. They think they know who the target was. Not her," he said as though Celeste couldn't hear him. "That's all I know." He lifted the mug to his mouth, took a sip as though testing the hotness of it, then drank it down.

"More?" Joyce asked.

"Nope, gotta go. Just wanted to make sure everything was okay here. You got your suitcase?" Only after he asked the question did he look at Celeste again.

She nodded. "Thanks."

He stood and headed for the door, Joyce followed him. Celeste wondered if he had ever seen Joyce like she was at the Huntington, dancing in front of the painted ladies.

She thought back to the interviews at the airport. It was easier to say she had fainted. She almost had. The dead woman had Celeste's passport, Celeste would be listed among the dead. Now no one would be looking for her. That was the idea.

When Joyce came back, Celeste had refilled their mugs, and had taken Biff's to the kitchen.

"He's had a rough life." Joyce shook her head with a look of sadness. "Now let's get you started on your life path. Your new life. So whatever you did before, now you have to do something different."

"I really need to exercise."

"Okay, good, that's a start. Whatever kind of exercise you did before, we have to pick out something that's not the same."

"I did Zumba at the Y."

"Zumba is out. Y is out. What about running?"

Celeste thought for a moment. "Power walking. I've never done that."

"Good, good. I'll check on that. Now what about a job? Something you've wanted to do—"

"Flower arranging. I've always wanted to do that."

"A class, maybe. I'll check on that. Want to work for a florist?"

"Sure."

Joyce looked down at her notepad. "What would you like to do for fun? Nothing you did in your old life."

"Didn't do much for fun. I want to go to the movies. See everything that's going to be nominated for awards."

"Lots of theaters around. You can power walk there so you won't need transportation." Joyce smiled. "I'll get started on checking things out." She closed her notebook and unfolded a sheet of paper. "Your job today is cleaning the floors in this house. It's not hard and I'll show you what we usually do. We get inspected occasionally, never know when. We've always passed and I want to keep it that way. Reflects on me. So the floors will give me a good rating. You're doing it for me."

Dinner was heavenly lasagna that Molly made. "It's very easy," she told Celeste. "I'll teach you how to make it."

"Okay," Celeste said, and hoped that the opportunity never came up. Although she would like to be as admired as Molly was. Even if Molly showed her all her trade secrets, Celeste didn't think it would turn out as well.

After dinner, Joyce had set up everything for Celeste. She could power walk with a group who met at Blair High School's track early every morning. It was just a few blocks south of where they were. There was a flower arranging class taught by a professional at the local Senior Center so she could get college credit. The next day, early, she assisted a florist in bringing back the flowers bought at the Flower Mart in downtown L.A.

Celeste was overwhelmed at the speed that Joyce had made all the arrangements, and she tried to convey her enthusiasm. The only flaw in the program was going downtown L.A. where she might be seen. But at 2 in the a.m. wearing her wig and all the brown clothes in Edna's wardrobe, she should be okay. If she wasn't, then all her problems would be over and she wouldn't have to worry any more.

An employee in a van that was lettered *Delacey Florists*, picked up Celeste in the early morning darkness. Little traffic. The woman only nodded to her as she climbed in the van, then drove to the entrance of the Arroyo Parkway off Glenarm. Everyone called it the Pasadena Freeway. It had originally started as an elevated bikeway six miles to Los Angeles when the bicycle craze was at its height in the early 1900s. The right-of-way became the freeway it was now.

They exited in Chinatown on Broadway and continued to the Flower Mart. The woman said nothing the entire time, not even 'good morning.' That was okay with Celeste. She sure didn't feel like talking. Then she wondered if the woman knew who lived in the house and thought they were all criminals. Some of the Wit-Secs were—telling all for a lighter sentence and to escape fatal reprisals. Maybe she thought Celeste was a battered wife, and was going to tell her in detail about all of her suffering. Maybe it was the other way around and the woman had her own mental devils to deal with.

Celeste decided just to go along, literally, for the ride. The woman would tell her what she wanted her to do.

At the Mart, lots of people, lights, and, of course, flowers. The smell of freshness perked Celeste up. The woman went from vendor to vendor, seemingly purposeful. Sometimes the vendors gave her flowers, as though they knew what she wanted. Maybe they had been ordered online by the florist. Or she bought the same thing each time. Celeste followed pushing a cart that was getting fuller and fuller with each stop.

Then she saw him.

Her nightmare a reality. Celeste kept her head down, the floppy brim of the brown felt hat hiding her face. She bent over a little, leaning on the cart as though it was a walker. She didn't know if the man looked at her or not, but suddenly he turned—she could see the bottom half of his body—and the shoes as they abruptly walked away. What did that mean? Had he recognized her? Getting someone to come and kill her for real?

She stood hunched over the cart, shaking. Also it was cold. As though the woman could read her mind, she led Celeste to the coffee stand, bought two Long Johns and coffees and gave her one of each. They stood, eating, drinking and looking around. Celeste careful not to raise her head too high so that her face was visible.

The woman still had not spoken to her. Celeste was just glad not to have to make small talk. Maybe the woman had done this before with former residents and knew she wasn't supposed to ask questions.

When they returned to the house it was still dark. Celeste was barely out of the van when another person almost pushed her aside and got in. Marcie. One of house's inmates and not a friendly one.

Celeste just stood for a second, surprised. Was Marcie working at the florist's? When she got to the gate, she realized Marcie hadn't left it open, but Celeste had a key.

She went back to bed and slept for over two hours. When she went down to breakfast, Joyce, white-faced, took her aside and said. "You were lucky. Just after she dropped you off, someone rammed her van."

Celeste gasped. So she had been recognized. "Marcie was with her. Were they hurt?"

"Both in the hospital. The other driver was killed. Couldn't happen to a nicer guy—whoever he was. I'll be in touch with the hospital, and let you know."

Celeste busied herself pouring a cup of coffee, slopping over the sides of the mug and onto the counter, her mind splintered with thoughts, her hands shaking. Too scary.

Joyce didn't have anything planned for them today since Celeste was up so early, but suggested they do some laundry, her job for the day. That meant picking up all the pillowcases full of sheets and towels from each of the bungalows and apartments. At the same time they gave out clean sets.

Celeste was able to see what all the accommodations were. The little bungalows were original with built-in dark wooden buffet with drawers at the bottom and glass-enclosed doors in the dining room. The same type of cabinets in the kitchen. The windows were all set in matching dark wood. And the fireplace, Batchelder-designed tiles framing it with cabinets on both sides the height of the mantelpiece. Very compact, vintage California Bungalow architecture. She loved it, awed by the originality.

Two days later, Celeste learned that the woman who had driven her to the flower mart had been rammed into by her ex-husband. He had been stalking her. Both women were going to be okay. Celeste was more relieved than she could say—no one was stalking her after all.

With the two women away, Celeste got more time at the florist's shop which meant she was picked up very early in the morning. She enjoyed working with the flowers—preparing arrangements, although she was doing mostly prep work or replicating bouquets already designed.

She liked her flower arranging class also. She still had to choose a purpose in her life. Otherwise why had she risked doing what she did, taking the dead woman's passport, false though it was. To be able to pay rent on her own accommodation somewhere, she had to develop some sort of skill unrelated to what she had before.

And she had to get her mind back in working order. Her thoughts felt scattered. She found it hard to concentrate. She could only attribute that to shock. How long would this state go on? She needed a magic wand to make everything okay again. At least her mind all right, not under a state of siege as it had been in her life before—before she became Edna.

Her rosy future came to a halt when Biff picked her up to go to an FBI interview. It was in a bare room in an office building at Colorado and Marengo in Pasadena. A man and a woman. They wanted her to testify at the trial. Celeste realized it had to do with why Edna was on the Wit-Pro Program. She scrambled to answer. She had no idea what Edna or whatever her name had been—could testify to. "I need to see what I said before, to refresh my memory, I've been in such a daze."

They didn't seem sympathetic, but they accepted what she said. They didn't seem disappointed either. That puzzled Celeste. She couldn't tell what they really wanted.

"We know you've been through quite a bit," the woman said. "Another person at the airport has completely lost her memory. Others are having difficulty coping. Perhaps we need to get a therapist for you." Her voice trailed off.

God! No!

The woman didn't seem to be enthusiastic about that idea, looking at the man for his reaction. He shrugged. Celeste didn't say anything, almost holding her breath. The two had a brief whispered discussion. The meeting seemed to be pointless, but the two seemed to be satisfied.

Then they segued into her testimony at the airport. It was general, just verifying her statement, and being assured that she saw nothing that would help in the investigation. The woman stated that this was not their case but they were helping out since they had come to talk to her about testifying in the future.

Then Biff took her home. He said nothing on the short drive. Celeste could easily have walked it. She said 'thank you' and got out. He still said nothing.

Mr. Delacey's florist operation was a small warehouse on North Lake that operated like a factory. It had a parking lot in front, and small shop for the public. He had contracts with all of the large hotels, as well as Cal Tech and its Athenaeum, The Huntington Library, and other classy venues that put on elegant galas and weddings. She realized that the trips to the Flower Mart had only been to pick up exotic flowers for special arrangements. A large truck brought the bulk of the flowers.

Mr. Delacey also had contracts with a variety of well-to-do families who liked to have flower throughout the house. Celeste learned that he had worked at the White House doing floral arrangements and his contacts and prestige from there resulted in contracts. She was happy to be working with happy things—flowers. Most of the people there were too busy working, meeting deadlines to have time to chit-chat. Breaks were sporadic, as was lunch, usually eaten while working. Celeste had no complaint as they might work a ten-hour day then be off for a day or so when there were no orders to fill. She liked the schedule.

About a week into the hectic pace, her boss gave her the assignment to assist a driver going to the Santa Anita Racetrack, now setting up the flowers for a large gala there. Celeste caught her breath and was about to ask that someone else go, but she didn't. The possibility of seeming him there was high. More than high, like highly probable.

It was his milieu. Celeste had wondered how much he had to do with the high incidence of the horse deaths there. Horse racing may kill, but there was always someone for hire to eliminate the competition. She consoled herself with the hat and the wig. Floral arrangers did not fit any stereotype. So Celeste blended in. but that didn't stop her heart rate from accelerating. Raoul, the driver, also a floral designer, was slim, short, not the type to stop an attack on her, but rather somebody who could be gobbled up by a coyote. She squelched her thoughts. They were going to be in the Club House. He would be in the stables murdering horses. He would never see her.

Before they left the flower factory, Raoul picked up a few discarded flowers—the stems too short, or past their shelf life, and deftly wove them into the band on her hat. She caught her reflection in the window. Definitely livened up the drab hat. Maybe that wasn't such a good idea—too noticeable—but the flowers made her feel good.

Santa Anita was about a twenty-minute drive, actually half an hour by the time they reached the loading dock of the Club House to set up in the Chandelier Room. She kept looking around every time someone came into the cavernous room. It was beautifully decorated, with a high, maybe a two-story ceiling and, of course, the famous chandeliers for which the room was named.

Raoul glanced at her several times, annoyed. Her constant looking around was slowing them down—his look said. She stopped worrying. If he came in, there were others there—dusting, cleaning the floor, setting up tables. Her hat and wig disguised her, but she realized she was the only woman in the room and stood out because of her hat—the flowers on it. Too late now. She kept working.

She became absorbed in the beauty of the flowers and how the vases, urns actually, were enhancing the room. How could she feel anything but happy around the flowers? Finally they were finished, and Raoul, the perfectionist, was pleased. She sighed with relief. Now they could get out of there.

"I want to make a bet."

Celeste took a minute before she realized what he meant. "I'll wait here."

"No, come with me. It's on the way to the van."

She followed him. He knew how to get to the betting booths. She stood beside him as he talked to the clerk. They seemed to know each other. A man came in crooning, but not well. He seemed not well, as he was staggering. Drunk, Celeste assessed, then she realized who it was. It was *him*. She froze. The man moved nearer in her direction. *Oh, my beautiful baby*....

Celeste quickly shifted to the other side of Raoul, pulling her hat brim down and leaning into Raoul's shoulder. Deterred, he began to sing to the woman behind them. The woman backed away and went to the other clerk who was now free. When she did that, he moved with her. "I'm next, bitch" in a slurred voice. But the clerk was already working on the woman's transaction.

He pulled a gun.

It wavered as he aimed it at the woman.

Celeste screamed. Raoul saw what was happening, dashed for the door on the other side of the betting booths, pulling Celeste with him. They pushed through the door and down the hallway, Raoul still pulling her. As they ran, two security officers came running from the opposite direction and passed them heading toward the betting booths.

They ended up in the Chandelier Room again, Raoul leading her out toward the van. When they were driving off, Raoul said, "You're sure an exciting date."

Date?

"Just kidding. Women aren't my thing. No offense."

Celeste laughed out of sheer nervousness. *Date?* "Remind me not to come back here again."

"It sure won't be with me, honey. Can't wait to tell the boss. We should get a bonus. Hazard pay."

But that wasn't the end of it. The Arcadia Police, the jurisdiction the racetrack was in, called on Raoul to testify as to what he saw. They wanted her also, but Raoul told them that the woman who was with him was not quite all there, didn't hear or see well, and had her face buried in his shoulder while he was making the bet as she was afraid of people. Celeste considered the last part to be true. He had given them a fictitious name, so now Celeste had two false names. The police decided that they didn't need her for a witness as they had Raoul and the woman who had moved to the betting window, and another man who had just entered the room when he pulled the gun. Plus the two betting clerks.

That bump in the road was overcome, much to Celeste's relief. But she saw another in the offing. The gun. She was sure it was the gun she had shot her husband with. Her brother-in-law had left it on the kitchen table, safety off, not the Celeste knew anything about that or about guns at all. When her husband had staggered toward her, menacing—she knew the look—she grabbed the gun and when he was about to hit her with his hammy fists, she pulled the trigger. She also didn't know that it was an automatic and kept firing as long as she held the trigger. The recoil stitched bullets up and down his body. He was about as dead as dead can be. Her brother-in-law grabbed the gun out of her hand. And that's when she left for the airport—no destination in mind just away, away, away.

He had seen it all and now had the gun. He didn't care about his dead twin brother. It wasn't the case of the good twin and the evil twin. Both were evil—Celeste had learned too late.

Were her prints still on the gun? Maybe not if he had handled it a lot. But the bullets could be matched with the ones in her now-dead unloving husband. Even if the prints were matched to her, her passport showed her as having been shot at the airport. What if they ran the prints of the dead woman?

She couldn't worry about that now. She was not out of the frying pan, and hopefully not into the fire. Only time would reveal that ominous secret.

At work, Raoul was more solicitous of her. He was, maybe, ten to fifteen years younger than her, but he treated her now like a baby sister. He joked and made her laugh. She hadn't done a lot of laughing for a while. It felt good, and good to work with the flowers. Flowers only brought happiness.

He wasn't always there and she wasn't always partnered with him when they made deliveries and set-ups. But now she had a legitimate reason to refuse to go to Santa Anita Racetrack. She wondered if any horses had died while her brother-in-law was locked up. She became more interested in the deaths of the racing horses—as the average was way above that for any racetrack—and for Santa Anita, too. Why was that? She watched for news of any horse dying while he was in jail. She didn't want to leave any trace of her research in the computers at her residence or at the florist. She occasionally asked Raoul if the maniac was still in jail. He researched on his phone and kept her up-to-date. Thankfully, nothing to report.

She thought about *that* night. She had been trying to suppress all memory—but the idea came to her—what if her brother-in-law had left the gun out for just that purpose. That she would pick it up to defend herself. Continuing the thought—what if Homer had deliberately provoked her husband? Did he want to get rid of his twin brother? She knew he had designs on her, but she never knew what the brothers' relationship really was. They were always arguing. They were identical twins, so there had to be some bond between that that she didn't understand.

If her brother-in-law needled him, her husband would never hit him—only her. It didn't matter who had got him riled up, he took it out on her.

The fraction of the second it took her to size up the situation at the time and realize the gun would be a defense against more pain—

She turned those thoughts off. Her brother-in-law was capable of doing that. But why? Even if she knew, it might not make any sense to her.

Celeste hadn't yet been able to meet with the power walkers at the Blair High track. They met at first light and usually before that Celeste was picked up by someone from the florist's to work on the fresh flowers arriving there for orders that day. The few days she'd had off, she'd slept through breakfast.

Joyce had made contact with the group and they were willing to welcome her whenever she could meet with them. Celeste guessed they knew about the home that Joyce managed.

Finally, a morning arrived that Celeste could meet them. It was cold enough for the watchman's knit cap and gloves that Joyce gave her, along with a water bottle. In fact, Joyce had a whole shelf of them in the kitchen.

Celeste walked the few blocks to the track. She saw a group loosely assembled and approached them. One woman stepped away and toward her, the others smiling. Celeste put a smile on her face. Sometimes she forgot to do that.

"Hi, you must be Edna." For a split second, Celeste was about to turn around to look for the person named Edna. Then she realized that was her. She put out her hand and the woman shook it.

"Joyce emailed me that you might be coming over. We've been expecting you." She didn't say it with a question, more as a welcome.

"Hi. I'm here now. I'm a complete novice. All I know about power walking is that you put one foot in front of the other." Celeste tried to sound light-hearted. She wanted them to like her. Female friends had been lacking in her life for quite a while.

"That's the main thing," she said. "We're training for our next 10K. Some of us have done those before, but there are others like you who are starting from scratch, working up to it. We call ourselves the Power W, Walkers." She waited, as though for Celeste's question. Then Celeste got it. "What is the W. for?" that's what the woman was waiting for. "Power Women Walkers," she said with a laugh.

Celeste smiled and nodded—still the bobbing head.

The woman introduced 'Edna' and each gave her name, none of which Celeste remembered as they went around. About eight in the group. Some were hugging take-out coffee cups.

"All the newbies have a mentor, a big sister actually. I'll be yours, if you want." The woman seemed unsure of what Celeste's answer would be.

"I'd appreciate that. That means trainer, too, right?"

"Okay, let's get started. I'm setting my timer. Let's go." All the women started walking. "We start off slow. Walk normally for ten steps, then power walk. I'll show you how. Take it easy and built up your stamina. We do about eight miles an hour."

Celeste knew that regular walking was three miles an hour, about twenty minutes a mile. *Whew*. But she wanted to do it. She was definitely huffing only after a few sequences. They used the track for an hour before the Blair High School students started arriving for their training in various sports. At the end of the hour she wished someone would drive her the few blocks home. She certainly wasn't going to power walk it.

On her way back she thought about her brother-in-law, Homer. She wanted to know where he was at—was he still in jail or was he going to pop up somewhere. She had to get the info from Raoul. But she didn't want to ask him too often because he might wonder why she was so curious.

What if Homer, now with plenty of time on his hands, went over the scene at the racetrack and realized who she was. He might not have read her name in the news as being one of those shot at the airport, so he might not know that she was 'dead.' If he realized it was her it wouldn't take long for him to find out where she worked, stalk her and follow her home.

She sighed a moan. Her new life was not simple. All she wanted to do was go back to her room, crawl into bed to hide. But there'd be breakfast with the group, then chores. Joyce had mentioned another outing. That would take her mind off her present problems.

The Allendale branch library was across the street from Blair. Dare she get a library card? She had read a lot as a child. Now she didn't have much time for reading—certainly not to put her to sleep at night, as she was usually so tired she was out at the same second the light was.

There was something about a library that brought peace to her. She remembered in her childhood a big room full of books that made her feel happy, content—and safe. She didn't remember where it was, not the house she lived in, but she remembered running her hand along the rows of spines of the books as she walked around the room. That's all she remembered—a fragment and a feeling.

As Celeste unlocked the gate, she smelled coffee—and all along the walkway other smells of maple syrup, eggs frying. When she entered the house some greeted her as she hung up her jacket on the clothes tree and stuffed the gloves into the pockets. She didn't often eat with them as she left so early for the florist's. They knew that.

Then in the evenings she went up to her room after dinner, tired. On non-work days she joined them in the evenings in the Gathering Room.

The four teenagers, each from a different families, were huddled together, almost clinging to each other—three girls and a boy. She knew they went to Blair. A few of the children played games in the room, the toddlers off to bed. Most of the women sat at the table chatting. Joyce worked the large picture of Venice's Grand Canal. Celeste suspected that some of the pieces were missing or traded with pieces from other puzzles because it hadn't been finished yet. Joyce wasn't the only one who tried her hand at it. No radio or TV in the room, and the teens weren't pulling out their phones every few seconds as they didn't have any.

Tonight she'd had cleaning and dishwashing duties and had finished with those, content to just sit in a rocker-type chair and watch the children.

At the florist's the next morning, Raoul told her that the race-track gunman was out on bail. She was surprised. "Must have a pricey lawyer," Raoul said. That meant she had to be more wary. Her stomach felt like an elevator that had free-fallen fifty stories. Raoul seemed to be as upset as she felt. She wondered why. Then she realized that Homer knew who had been the witnesses to his gun-waving. Was he going to try to eliminate them all? If he came around, would he recognize her even in the wig? He would play with her like he was the cat and she was the mouse. He would 'tease' her cat-like saying he was going to report how she murdered her husband. He was fiendish. She had no defenses against him. How was she going to get out of this?

"Get someone to move your van to the loading dock," Celeste told him. Raoul seemed indecisive, looking one way and then another as though he didn't know which way to go. Then she thought *he doesn't*.

"Disguise yourself somehow. Make yourself fatter." He couldn't do taller, but he was so thin, he would be instantly recognizable. Even a wig wouldn't help him.

He bounced up and down like a little boy needing the bathroom.

"I'll switch routes." He headed for the supervisor.

Celeste continued cutting the stems the way he wanted them. Not all the same length so the would be at different heights in the vase.

He came back, his agitation abated. "It's okay. I go out later from the loading dock. Worked out perfectly." He smiled. "Do more of the iris. Maybe six." He gave her some other instructions about what flowers to get from the cooler, and the lengths.

The attack took place the next morning, still dark. Homer was waiting when Raoul drove in and parked. Others were arriving. Homer sprang from his hiding place and hit Raoul with a wrench. Celeste saw it and yelled. Others ran to Raoul, someone called the police and an ambulance. Homer was trapped between two cars with all of them around him—seven people able to identify him. Homer waved the wrench like a sword in front of him, keeping everyone away. The group consisted of a former soldier, two hefty and strong drivers, and a woman who was a former Marine and could have taken Homer on herself. Raoul was well-liked, so Homer wasn't going to get out of the parking lot easily.

Celeste wished she had a weapon. Suddenly an idea came to her and she ran to the back door, reaching inside for the fire extinguisher, yanking it from the rack. They'd all been trained on using it. She pulled the pin from the ring. The clanging of the extinguisher against the buttons of jacket made a noise and Homer turned

She sprayed him like a cockroach. He staggered and lurched toward her, she side-stepped and kept the nozzle toward him until he was covered with white foam. She realized she was coughing from fumes. No one else came close.

A police car drove into the lot and within seconds two guns were on Homer. Then a paramedics truck was directed to where Raoul lay.

One of the officers motioned to Celeste to back away. She realized she was still holding the fire extinguisher and set it down. She was finished. They didn't need her anymore. She went into the building to get some water. The chemical from the spray was choking her and her eyes were watering. She hoped Homer was even worse off.

Later they learned Raoul had a broken arm from warding off the wrench and had a head injury but no permanent damage. In a week he was back, arm in a sling. a bandage around his head, and about as buoyant as he could be. No one was after him now.

Homer was charged with attempted murder of Raoul. Another charge of wielding the gun in public, but they couldn't charge him with attempted murder on that one as there were no bullets in the gun or on him. Obviously the intent was not there.

But the interesting turn of events was that the police had a gun to match up with the bullets from his dead twin brother. After test firing the gun, Homer was arrested for the murder of his twin brother.

Homer had taken the gun from her and kept it. The chances were that her fingerprints were obliterated. What did he tell the police when they came after the shooting? Or did he run away also and let someone else find the body? If the police had been looking for her—the spouse is always the prime suspect—then they would have written her off their list when they found out she had been shot at the airport.

Celeste smiled. She was glad Homer always did dumb things.

A few weeks later, gleefully Raoul showed Celeste the news article on his phone.

She read:

The defense argued that the defendant saw his sister-in-law shoot her husband, who was his twin brother, and that he wrestled the gun away from her before she could shoot him or take her own life.

The prosecution argued that at the time of the brother's shooting, the wife was at the airport, herself being shot in the shooting spree, therefore the real murderer of the brother was his twin, the defendant, not the wife.

~The End~

DEPARTURES

Sonja is at LAX when a shooting occurs triggering her memory of her last visit to Lido. She recalls the meeting of her upstairs neighbors, and what happened that summer. Sonja recalls all of this as she waits at LAX for a flight that may, or may not, take her back to Lido for her annual summer vacation.

Sonja leaned against the thick pillar to adjust her sock. It was all bunched up in her shoe. How did that happen?

She'd been to LAX at least once every year for the past twenty. Always there was construction, remodeling going on—like the Winchester house in Northern California when its owner was alive—the renovation couldn't stop. Sonja had to check in at one terminal and the take a shuttle to another, as though passengers were inconveniences. Once in the airport she was just a sheep in a flock being herded through the chutes.

She heard a loud noise, and then a sting on her cheek like the bite of a bee. She jerked back and touched her check.

Blood.

She looked at the pillar and saw a piece gouged out, a piece that hit her. But what caused it to fly off like that? She felt weak and wanted to sit down. She grabbed the handle of her carry-on and pulled it, moving away from the pillar at the back of a row of seats.

For a moment she just stood and stared. No one in sight. What? Just a few minutes ago the place was full of people. Then she realized all of the colored cloth on the floor was the clothing of people lying down, crouching.

Suddenly there was shouting and she saw two people with "Security" on the jackets running in the same direction. Sonja sat down.

More people in uniform were running—EMTs, LAPD, Airport Security.

Sonja sat behind the two large cement pillars, her arms wrapped around the long handle of her carry-on as though for protection. People were getting up, moving away from where the uniforms were. Two EMTs came walking toward her, scanning the group. One stopped beside her. "Let me take a look at that," he said.

At first Sonja didn't know what he meant, then she realized her cheek had bled. He set his case down and began to pull out items.

The other EMT walked around asking in anyone was hurt.

Her EMT cleaned the blood away, the antiseptic stinging as though she was being struck again by the chipped plaster. "You won't have a scar, it's just a scratch." He put on ointment and then a wide piece of gauze and taped it down.

"You can take that off tonight." He closed up his case and took out a small clipboard. "I need your name."

Sonja's mouth felt glued shut. She unzipped her jacket pocket and pulled out her passport and handed it to him. He recorded the information and handed the passport back to her. "Stay here for a while. You've had a little shock. You might feel dizzy if you get up right away."

Sonja tried to smile, tried to say 'thank you,' but she couldn't make her commands work. The bandage seemed to hold her cheek in place. She didn't feel the scratch.

The other EMT called to him. He stood, patted her on the shoulder, "Take care, Sonja."

Sonja still sat after the EMT left her. Some people were moving back to their seats, most silent, a few whispering to each other. All seemed to be in shock as she was. She thought about where she was going—Lido in Venice. She went every year, renting one floor of a house that sat between a police station and a classy Inn.

She stayed a month each time, walking around the island and sketching. In the mornings she sat looking out of the large front window, drinking coffee. There wasn't much to see. Trees and greenery on the other side of the road which hardly had any traffic. Except for the police cars, and of them. There were elegant old houses on the short street. One side street off of it that was only a block long.

Sonja never learned the history of how the streets came to be, but definitely they were not in a grid pattern.

For the last few years, maybe four, a young man and an older man had lived on the floor above her. The older man, not much older in his 30s, the younger one in his 20s, seemed more like a caregiver to the younger on. A companion, perhaps, was a better word.

They went out for a walk every morning, no set time, but Sonja could see them as she sat drinking coffee.

Once, the young man had stopped in the road in front of the house and wouldn't go any farther, even though his companion urged him on. The young man acted, as Sonja could only describe, like he was having a tantrum. He jumped up and down, waving his arms, doing a dance to music in his head. The companion leaned against the stone pillar at the end of the fence that separated the property from the Inn. He, theatrically, because Sonja felt she was watching a play, pulled out a package of cigarettes from his sweater pocket, took one out, tapped it on the package, put the package away, pulled out a lighter from the other pocket and lit the cigarette protruding from his mouth.

He casually smoked it, paying no attention to the younger man. Still in frantic movement, looked at the trees across the road, at the sky and in different directions, all his movements done slowly. But he never looked at the young man who stayed in place as though on a small platform doing his gyrations.

Sonja had sketched them, together and separately, on the pages of her small sketchbook.

They had never spoken to her, but presumably knew about her. She had the impression from the agent she rented from that the parents had bought the building a few years ago. But she didn't know for sure and wasn't that interested to ask questions. She wasn't here to get involved in other people's lives while she was on vacation. She was barely coping with her own life.

Then suddenly the younger man would stop, stand still in place. The older man, by this time had finished his cigarette, put it out on the heel of his shoe and then placed it in a small container in his pocket. Sonja liked that in him.

Then he offered his left elbow to the younger man who grasped his upper arm as though he was blind, and they walked off toward Fontane, making a right, and then to Via Gallo, the main street, and a left over the canal. She had seen them one day, and imagined that they were following the same route.

Sonja often heard them leaving, going down the stairs, and sometimes heard them return after lunchtime. She guessed they had lunch somewhere. She didn't know what they did for dinner because they never went out again.

She thought about following them. Then realized what a shocking idea that was—like stalking. No, she would only do it once. It wasn't like her to think that way—follow someone.

She quickly gathered her things before she could consider the idea further. She followed the route she thought they had taken. At Via Sandro Gallo, she made a left over the canal—not a large one, but one that took private motor boats and water taxis. Past the pharmacy on the other side of the street where there were also a few small shops.

Not many people out walking, it was Sunday. She would be noticed if the older of the two had turned around a few times, but he never did. She slowed down leaving a large distance between them. A few stores on both sides, but nothing open. Apartments and large ornate homes here, a residential area. Tourists didn't frequent here.

The two crossed Via Gallo and walked down a side street. Sonja continued on, crossed the road and then doubled back to the side street they had taken. It led to a long narrow park on the water side with benches and a path than went alongside the water about ten feet above it. No beaches.

There were concrete tables about the size of a card table with stone seats. The top had a design for chess or checkers. Sonja had seen them in other European parks.

The two men sat down and began to play. She wasn't close enough to see what the game was. She walked on to a bench out of their sight but she could still glance over to see if they were still there. The younger man seemed in his element, concentrating on the game. Sonja wondered if he could perhaps be a *savant.*

She sat and sketched, only occasionally glancing at the men to make sure they were still there. Their concentration on the game was surprising to her. Also surprising was the amount of wildlife that came out and performed for her since she sat there without moving much. She sketched everything—the squirrels, birds, lizards, and also the boats plying back and forth. She was lost in her world, an inner peace which she always had here on Lido, sketching.

She saw a movement at the table and turned slightly to see them get up. Again the older of the two offered his elbow and the younger man grasped the upper part of his arm. Then they walked back the way they had come from Via Gallo and made a right. It had been two hours. When Sonja got to the corner she couldn't see them, but she walked in the direction they had taken. There was a small restaurant a few doors away and when she went past she saw them inside.

Across the street was a gelato place, so she decided to go back to the park, eat the sandwich she had brought and then have a gelato for dessert. From there she would be able to see when they left. She sat on a different bench in the park, near the water and sketched the myriad of boats for twenty minutes then left.

She ordered a Nutella gelato that was a mixture of hazelnuts and chocolate, and sat at a small table where she could look into the restaurant's large front window. The sign read *Barbarigo's*.

The two were still sitting there, the young man facing her. A much older man with a fringe of white hair sat with them. He seemed to be telling a story, gesturing. The young man sat rigid, staring straight ahead and could have looked into Sonja eyes from across the street.

She knew he couldn't see her because his stare was unseeing. The caregiver was laughing, enjoying the older man's raconteuring, if that was what it was.

Sonja reflected back to when the two were playing the game in the park. The younger man seemed animated, involved in the game, perfectly normal. Perhaps that's why his caregiver took him there. Now, at the restaurant, he was back in his catatonic state. The old man, got up and went behind the counter, moving around. Then he came back to the table and set down two cups of espresso, but he didn't join them again.

Sonja wondered if the older man was related to the caregiver, or at least a friend, or had become friendly with them if the two went to lunch there every day. It was a piece of mundane information that she wasn't about to pursue. She finished her gelato as the two men rose and left the restaurant. They turned toward home.

She crossed the street to look at the menu posted in the window of every European restaurant. Home cooking, she thought. She might try it but probably not for lunch if that's where her upstairs neighbors came every day.

She stopped following them. She wondered why she was curious. Well—she really didn't have anything else to do. And that was the way she wanted it. Let her mind float, sketch, no commitments. It was a restorative period for her. She needed it as much as her clients did.

Back in her apartment she made coffee, sat in the living room, again looking out of the front window. She flipped through her sketchbook, now full. Sonja studied the sketches of the young man. She could read different things in each—when he was playing chess or checkers, in front of the house, and at the restaurant. She looked at the eyes as she had sketched them, with no touching up now. They all said different things. Who was this person?

Then she realized she was trying to figure him out. He was not one of her clients.

She wanted to know what was in his head. Was it possible for anyone to find out? She highly doubted it. He was in another world, not one that she or those like her could go to. She wondered how much mental pain he was in. She hoped none, but from his actions and her experience, she thought he had some pain. She feared it was a lot, and doubted that she or anybody could help him just by talking.

She looked through the sketchbook again, then she put it on the end table and went to get another one from her suitcase. This time she picked a larger one. It wouldn't fit into her green bag—a purchase at the Biennale—but it had ties on it so she could attach it to the straps of her bag.

Back in her chair, sipping coffee, Sonja thought about inviting the two to dinner. It wouldn't be an altruistic offer. She knew herself— she wanted to study the young man, see what was in his head. Only the caregiver would enjoy dinner, the young man would sit staring. He would eat, she was sure, but quickly, almost like an animal, gobbling the food up in a few seconds.

She knew the dinner would be for her, not for them.

She awoke from a dream. She had asked the two to dinner. Afterwards the caregiver had made advances, hugged her too tightly for too long and she'd tried ot push him away. She must have cried out because the young man grabbed him from behind, gripping his upper arms and pulling him away from her, then flinging him down. The caregiver's head hit the table and she fell, dead.

Sonja was fully awake now. She looked for the interpretation of the dream. Was it a warning to her to leave well enough alone, not open the proverbial Pandora's box?

It was 4 a.m. She got up, made coffee, and brought it and the new sketchbook back to bed. She drew the scene as she remembered it. It was still vivid. Not like her other dreams that faded into mist as soon as she woke up.

Later she was relieved when she saw the two start out on their walk. The dream had been so real that she could still recall the details. She shivered, remembering the scene.

It was overcast and intermittently rainy, but the two set off with the caregiver holding the large black English-style umbrella—a bumbershoot, for sure. Sonja loved that word—so *Alice in Wonderland.*

She would do nothing. She was letting her professional curiosity encroach on her vacation, and if she acted, encroaching on other people's lives. Plus there was the question of ethics.

She only had an umbrella, a mundane American one, but she was going to set off also—in the opposite direction, go to the public beach near the town center and sketch. That was what she did during her vacation life. She had to pack up her professional curiosity with her filled sketchbook. *None of your business*, she told herself.

Sonja walked to the end of the short street, Via Dal Mazia—the name was almost longer than the street—right on Via Lorenzo Marcello to a main street that paralleled Gallo, then left. The avenue had a long name befitting its length, but was called Marconi by the locals. A walk of six blocks to the public beach at the end of Elisabetta Street, the main street of the town. Another long name, but a short street—Granviale S. Maria Elisabetta, meaning the Grand Way of Saint Maria Elisabetta. She'd walk it back to her apartment, making a rectangular route.

No fee today at the public beach. She sat in a rattan chair in the area that looked like a cocktail lounge with the furnishings but it was outdoors. The chairs were being wiped dry by a worker, perhaps from the food stand. It hadn't rained since she left but the clouds were pewter, no sun, the air damp and slightly chilly. Sonja had brought a thermos of coffee and a sandwich. Her green Biennale sack held quite a bit. Gelato might not be the right dessert today but she could walk to a bakery on Elisabetta.

She sketched the chairs and low tables, the few birds, the couple with two little girls. The pigeons were bold, unafraid of her shooing motions. Beyond the concrete platform that comprised the outdoor seating area was a wide swath of sand leading to the edge of the water. No one in the water or walking barefoot on the sand.

There was something about the air of the island she liked. She loved Venice, and the proximity delightful. She could stay on Lido in peace, or get on the vaporetto at the Elisabetta plaza and go to Venice, one stop away, or three stops to St. Mark's. That was another world, and she liked to be able to go back and forth when she wanted. The two worlds were so different and that was the fascinating part.

Another world was visiting the contemporary art exhibits of the Biennale, an event that occurred every two years. In the park, the first stop on the vaporetto was half of the venue for the exhibits. The park was deceptively large. A section had permanent buildings, each the size of a large house, and owned by different countries—the U.S., France, U.K. and others. Large buildings along the wide paved walkway had other countries exhibits, and individuals were able to rent spaces to show their works.

The Biennale exhibits were in two main venues—at the park, and in the Arsenale. Throughout the city in unused churches, Ca's or casas like the Fortuny one, and other buildings, artistes were able to use the spaces for galleries. The Arsenale was the former shipyard buildings, large, long where Venice had excelled in building ships. The buildings of the ship-yards were rustic artworks of their own dating from the middle ages.

All of the artwork was avant-garde, so new and beyond catego-rizing. Also performance art was available to view. There seemed to be no parameters as to what could be exhibited or done. It was a looking into a world of the possible that expanded the parameters of what art could be, to the definition of what art was. Surrealistic, the world of Dali, was the closest she could come to describe what she saw.

It was Sonja's other world. She marveled at what came out of the minds of other artists. She marveled on two levels—at the mind—for the mind was her profession, and at the art that was so creative. Ideas that she would never have conceived of, the use of unusual materials, and designs. All were so mesmerizing. She always came away dizzy, on mental overload. She had never considered being an artist, sketching was a way of relaxing to her—not a way of life as she knew she hadn't the talent for that, nor did she want to spend her time that way.

At the Lido beach, she was lost in her world until some laughing, shrieking children ran around her chair. Raindrops were falling on her head, she realized, and quickly gathered her things and dashed to the shelter where some others were standing. The children's exuberance lightened Sonja's mind as though the sun had come out, but it hadn't. *May you always be this happy*, she said to them mentally.

Sonja put up her umbrella and headed for the bakery. She felt chilly from the dampness. A cherry tart perhaps, and hot chocolate. This was the day for it. The hot chocolate was the real thing, melted chocolate it tasted like, not the powder stuff she bought in the market at home. Both were up to her expectations, and the little bakery warm with smells of other good pastries.

Fortified she set off to walk the block to Via Gallo and then home. She could have taken the bus but she wasn't in any hurry and she needed the exercise.

As she approached Fontane, she saw the two men coming over the canal. They would meet at the same time. There wasn't any place she could go—no shops, no side streets, except straight ahead.

"Hallo," the older of the two greeted her. "You live in our house on the ground floor."

Sonja must have had a look of horror on her face—as if she was back in her dream.

"We live on the first floor," the man hastened to explain, seemingly reacting to her expression. "My name is Eric."

Sonja had to adjust to the floor numbers as she considered she lived on the first floor, but here in Europe it was the ground floor, and the first, was indeed, above her. "Oh, yes, now I recognize you."

He commented about the weather. The younger man gripped Eric's upper arm, and stared straight ahead, not looking at Sonja.

"Do come to lunch with us. Say, tomorrow? At 12:30? We eat early to avoid the crowd."

Sonja realized that Italians and other Europeans usually ate lunch at 1, not like Americans, like her, who ate at noon.

Eric gushed on because she hadn't said anything. "It's just up Via Gallo, called *Barbarigo's*. The food is very good." He paused, then said, "I'll give you the address." He waited for her reply.

Her mind was doing somersaults. This was what she wanted—to meet them and find out about the younger man, and now that she had it offered to her on a silver platter without her having to do anything—she didn't know what to do. Finally her brain kicked in and she said, "Yes, I'd love to join you. I know where the restaurant is. I'm glad to hear the food is good. I was thinking of eating there sometime. My name is Sonja."

"Hello, neighbor Sonja. Then it's settled. We'll meet you there tomorrow at 12:30. Shall we continue on?" They walked together to the house, the two men heading for the stairway door, on the left, and Sonja for her front door in the middle of the building. Eric waved as he ushered the younger man in.

Sonja stood still, lost in thought. Then a few raindrops reminded her to unlock her door and go in. *Tomorrow at 12:30 in a restaurant.* She actually had a luncheon date. If things didn't work out when they'd finished eating, she could say she had an errand some place so she didn't have to walk back with them. *Why was she even thinking about that?* She chided herself. *So negative.*

Then she realized, Eric hadn't introduced the younger man. And she wondered why. Did the younger man not want his name said aloud? It wasn't that Eric ignored him, Actually he was quite caring, making sure he didn't walk into a puddle, patting his hand as though to reassure him, talking to him as well as to her.

She didn't ponder about the younger man anymore. She'd find out tomorrow. Her curiosity, professional and personal, would be satisfied. She didn't think she wanted to spend time with the younger man, with or without Eric. That was her professional life and she had left that at home to come here each year to heal.

At the restaurant the two men were there first, even though she was five minutes early. Eric introduced her to the owner, Mr. Barbarigo. *The Italians sure know how to treat a woman, and he could have taught them all,* she thought as he ooohed and ahhhed over her. Eric enjoyed the scene thoroughly, laughing and clapping his hands at appropriate times, such as when Mr. Barbarigo brought her a rose in a small Murano glass vase. He told her to take it to remind her of him. She couldn't help but laugh, it was all so hokey—but welcomed. It had been a long time since anyone made a fuss over her.

They all had a good time—the three of them, but the third person was Mr. Barbarigo, as the young man sat as though deaf and blind. She was sure he was neither. Eric included him in the conversation. At first, Sonja tried to, but his unresponsiveness deterred her, so she directed her comments to Eric only, and then to Mr.Barbarigo who occasionally sat for a few minutes. The small restaurant was full, many take-out orders, or rather take-away as it was called here. He also had a lot of help who appeared when Sonja arrived, probably so that he could schmooze with the customers. Locals, Sonja thought, with some long-term visitors who came every year, as everyone seemed to know everyone else.

She had a most enjoyable time, with no thought of given her 'errand' excuse. She walked back with them staying on Eric's right as the young man had clamped his hand to Eric's left arm in the usual position. They mostly told each other amusing stories about their life. Sonja noted that Eric didn't reveal much about himself and neither did she. She learned nothing about the young man.

The lunch had been a success, but no mention of repeating it. Perhaps Eric felt it was too upsetting for the young man. She just didn't know.

But life went on for her as it did every year. One month, and it always went so quickly. Then she would spent eleven months reliving that month and looking forward to her next trip.

It was another blustery day, colder than yesterday, so Sonja turned on the heat. She had rarely felt the need to do that. The dampness was chilling. She was making coffee when she heard an unusual sound. It took her a minute to realize it came from the stairs.

She stood still and listened. The stairs. Clomp. Clomp. Clomp. She looked at the clock—10—so the two were going out for their regular routine.

But the clomping was sinister. A deliberate slamming down of his heavy boot in measured time. Was the young man showing his displeasure toward her? Did he think he was waking her up? Did he want her to know that he existed? That he was in charge?

Professionally what else could she do but interpret the action. She went into the living room to watch them leave.

They marched off, no 'dance' in the road today, but that was unusual when it occurred. Eric didn't seem as solicitous as usual. He didn't look at the younger man, or pat his hand. Didn't seem as animated.

Perhaps she was reading too much into the scene. Seeing what she wanted to see. Maybe it all had to do with the weather, not with her. She decided to stay in, get rid of the chill she felt. She had several books on her Kindle and there were others in the apartment. If the sun came out, she'd find a place for lunch, otherwise she wanted to remain sequestered—snug and warm and dry in her cozy apartment.

When they came back at their regular time, there was no clomping going up the stairs. Did the younger man feel it had 'punished' her enough? Or did he feel he no longer had to exert his power? Maybe he forgot the whole thing.

But the next morning he did the same thing. *Clomp. Clomp. Clomp.* Sonja felt a chill and not from the weather. She didn't have to fear Eric, she had to fear the younger man.

Whatever she did today, she would make sure she didn't run into them.

That night, she woke startled. A figure in the doorway of her bedroom. She could see him as the curtains let in the light from the walkways of the Inn and from the police station. She screamed. He didn't move. She knew it was him, the younger man. She couldn't see the expression on his face. He turned and walked away.

She shook so badly she couldn't move. Later, when she heard no more sound and felt a strong draft she went into the living room. Her front door was wide open. Now she was mad. How dare he? And just to scare her. Which he had completely. The final insult was to leave her door open. She knew she had locked it.

Then she heard running down the stairs. She slammed the door shut and locked it. Then a knocking. "Miss Sonja, Miss Sonja. Are you all right?" Eric.

She opened the door. He stood there, she could see him in the light, pjs, tousled hair, frantic. "He got the key. I am so sorry. I didn't realize they were the keys to this apartment. But his parents own the building…. I didn't know about the key. I am so sorry."

He went on, but she was assessing what he was saying. The younger man's parents owned the building. Of course they would have keys to the three apartments. The top one was empty so that's probably where they stayed. Not with their son.

"Here are all of the keys. I don't know what they're all for, but there are no others. Please, please is there anything I can do?" He hardly gave her a chance to respond. But she was in her nightgown and he was in his PJs and soon they were both shivering. She sent him on his way. What was the point of his going on with the same words? He obviously was very upset, which helped calm her down.

She made coffee and walked around the apartment. Nothing seemed to be out of place. Her purse was in the bedroom in the nightstand. But she knew he wasn't after that. If he had taken anything it would just be to make a statement that he could do anything he wanted. He could have kept another key, the one to the back door which was different, or maybe a duplicate to the front. No matter she would call the agent to have the locks rekeyed today. She couldn't call anyone now—2 a.m.

She took her coffee, climbed back into bed, and sketched what she remembered seeing. That helped, as though she was telling someone of the event. She made several sketches with different scenarios to alleviate the fear she had had.

She realized he was a cunning animal. His pose of stoicism was just a pose. He was a thinking human being. A dangerous one. She was no match for him and she was not going to be his prey. He played games. She wondered how much he toyed with Eric. Probably not much as he needed Eric. He would not be able to function without him. Where was Eric in all of this? Did he know what his charge was like? Eric seemed to be an innocent, unaware of his cunning roommate.

Mind playing. She didn't need that.

She was able to sleep for a few hours. No clomping today. A person came to rekey the locks. Naturally he arrived at 2, just when the two men were returning. She backed farther into the living room so they couldn't see her but she could see them. Eric gave a slight nod but it was behind the back of the young man whose eyes stared dead ahead.

She assessed her situation. She had a week more. She decided to spend some days in Venice, amid the crowds, to take her mind off of her neighbor upstairs. Now she understood why he was living here and not with his parents in the United States. Eric seemed American but he had a slight Italian accent, so she guessed he'd been raised here and then went to the U.S. probably as a child. Maybe he was even from Lido. But she decided she didn't want to know anything further.

Did she want to stay for the week? She could move to a hotel, but that was not the point of staying on Lido. It was to live here in an apartment like a resident. She wished she could have a conversation with Eric, but that seemed impossible. She didn't want to incur the wrath of the younger man, for she had no idea what he would do in retaliation. And she decided against informing the agent from whom she had rented the apartment. *Let sleeping dogs lie.*

The next morning the agent appeared. She told Sonja the two men upstairs had moved out, and she was arranging to have the place cleaned. She wanted Sonja to know that in case she wondered why people were going up and down the stairs and making noise in the flat above. Sonja invited her in for coffee and they sat at the kitchen table. It was more than just an FYI meeting as the woman had brought an assortment of pastries. More than the both of them could eat at one sitting.

Sonja guessed the woman knew about what had happened. Sonja had only told her she wanted the locks rekeyed immediately. Maybe Eric had told her. Maybe he wasn't an enabler after all, which she had considered. Sonja would tell her if the woman asked. But she never did. There were pauses in the conversation and the woman gave her openings but Sonja didn't relate what happened. The woman did ask about the new keys. And Sonja told her she would leave them when she left. She gave her the box of keys Eric had given her.

Sonja wanted to know more about the young man, but she didn't ask. She also wanted to know more about Eric and she did ask about him. The woman didn't know much, had only dealt with the owner. The two had lived here for the past two years after the parents had bought the house. The parents came separately to visit, the father staying longer, but the mother briefly.

Sonja felt the woman knew more than she was telling her, but Sonja didn't press her. "Where did the two go?" Sonja asked.

"They are staying at a hotel downtown for two days as that was the earliest they could get a flight back to the United States."

"So they are going home?" Two days. That meant she had to be wary for two days. She definitely didn't want to go downtown—but she would have to catch the vaporetto there. She wondered if the two were still going to have their game in the park and lunch at the same place.

"Yes, they were not expected to leave so soon. However, I can rent out the two apartments, as they are not coming back, and the parents don't intend to visit if their son is not here."

"Do you have anyone who is moving in?"

The agent shook her head. "We will clean first." Then she took her leave. Neither was getting all the information they hoped for was Sonja's impression.

She headed for Venice, glancing furtively around the plaza where the vaporettos docked. Each one arrived spewed out day trippers and residents with their dogs. There were so many people swirling around that Sonja thought it was futile for the two to see her as it was for her to see them.

She got off at the stop before St. Mark's and walked along the wide walkway taking in the ambiance, the kiosks, especially those of the artists. So many pictures of Venice and so many that she liked.

She found a place on the Grand Canal for lunch, sitting next to the water savoring the scene as much as the food.

Afterwards she sauntered around, her mind wandering as much as her feet. There was so much to see—a new exhibit at the Correr, Biennale art in various churches, and people watching. Definitely a world away from her Lido solitude.

She had a cappuccino, then climbed onto a crowded vaporetto, standing room only. But she always stood, except for a few times when she was able to sit in the prow and revel in the ride on the Grand Canal, one of her favorite excursions.

The sky was darkening, so she was glad she was heading back to her apartment. And glad that the two neighbors upstairs were gone. She took the bus as it looked more and more like it might rain.

The next day she did the same thing. Bought a small print of a scene of the Grand Canal, ate at a different restaurant and went into one of the churches to see an exhibit. The most interesting art was the artist's description of what he was trying to do. Of course, Sonja liked the mind part—what he thought and how he tried to capture the galaxy in a three-dimensional shiny sphere. Once she knew what the artist intended it to mean she could appreciate the piece.

Sonja spent the rest of week Monday through Thursday walking all over Lido, sketching, eating, stopping for a cappuccino or a gelato. The weight left her shoulders because the two were gone off the island, on their way home to the U.S. someplace. The cleaners may have come and gone in her absence, because no one came while she was there.

On Friday, her day to depart, she was having a last cup of coffee while looking out the front window. She saw the agent hurrying up. Sonja opened the door for her. The women's face was almost chalk-white as though she was wearing a different make-up.

But Sonja saw the woman wore no make-up. she sat down on the sofa and Sonja joined her. The woman grabbed her hand, Sonja almost jerked away, the woman's hands were ice.

"Eric, the older one, is missing. Since Sunday when they were scheduled to leave. The other one left, said nothing. Eric was supposed to go with him."

"Eric missing? What do you mean?" Sonja thought perhaps he'd had enough and had just left.

The woman bent her head, still clutching Sonja's hand in a steely grip. Then she looked up. "He was supposed to leave Sunday afternoon with that…that young man he was looking after." She bowed her head again, pulling out a handkerchief and wiping her eyes. "Monday morning the maid went in and all of his things were still there. Even his passport. So he didn't leave. And that other man said nothing to anyone." She squeezed Sonja's hand. "Be careful. Please be careful." Then she got up and hurried out.

Sonja went over the scene of what just happened. Incredible. So where was Eric? But Sonja knew, as did the agent, what happened to Eric.

So Sonja went home to Los Angeles and settled into her routine. She still thought about Lido and she still wanted to go back for her usual vacation.

About December she contacted the agent, ostensibly to wish her a Happy Holiday season, but asking about the availability of the apartment.

It was the same apartment she'd had for years, and it drew her. Even the appearance of that young man in the night hadn't totally spoiled it for her.

She had already analyzed that to death, how she felt, why she felt the way she did, ad infinitum. Even she came under her own scrutiny.

The agent didn't answer until the end of January. The apartment was available, possibly all three in the house at that time. The owners had divorced, so they might sell as their son wasn't coming back. All was undecided. Again, the agent said to come, she could guarantee her a very nice place.

Sonja thought about that. Perhaps a change would be good, another, better place. but the problem was she could only picture this place, picture herself in it again. Was it some sort of masochism, being there in the bedroom perhaps afraid that another person, or the son would appear to frighten her? Whey was she so intent on the same apartment? It was her home away from home, but wasn't it time she found a new one?

In her email, the agent said that Eric's body had been found about a month later, stuffed into a pipe in a canal.

She didn't elaborate. She didn't have to. 'Stuffed' meant that another person was involved. Sonja filed that information away in the Pandora's box she kept in her head for that type of information.

She had learned the younger man's name was Lionel, and somehow she was not thinking about him—remembering him standing in the doorway of her bedroom.

Now, at LAX, all of these thoughts crowded her mind. She was going to go to Lido, she was staying in the same apartment. The building was being sold.

~The End~

ARRIVALS

*Sybil arrives at LAX, but gets lost in the construction and stumbles into
the Departures area where she sees a man who shoots several people.
She runs and hopes no one finds out she was there and was a witness.*

ARRIVALS

The area Sybil found herself in, after following the disparate signs at LAX due to construction and remodeling or whatever, was crowded. People sitting, standing, moving around purposelessly. Long lines to go through Security. She realized she had wound up in *Departures*, not *Arrivals*. Chalk it up to her jetlag, lack of sleep and—

She noticed the young man a few feet away from her, in a long black coat and carrying a violin case. Sybil wondered if that was his 'carry-on,' because he didn't even have a backpack. The long black coat, not usually worn in summer in hot southern California, caught her eye. He was scanning the Security line, looking for someone, Sybil thought. He eventually saw the person. His next action was to set the violin case down. Sybil watched as he opened it and took out what looked like a machine gun. She wasn't standing far from him, but thought she must be seeing things.

He raised the gun, aimed and fired. Those standing fell, and others dropped at the sound. It was loud and grating.

Gunfire!

Get down, run.

Sybil reacted as she always did—ducking and getting away as fast as possible. She ran down the stairs, pulling her carry-on, backpack bumping.

She burst out of the automatic door before it had opened fully. Onto the sidewalk. A family was getting out of a taxi. Before the back door could be closed she slid in, surprising the man who almost closed it on her ankle.

"Take me to—" Sybil gave him the address. The taxi driver nodded and roared off, cutting across the lanes to the nearest exit. "First time here?" he asked. Sybil thought he was planning on taking the long route so she said, "Born here."

"Yeah, me, too." But it sounded like *Oh, sure, lady, tell me another one.*

He said nothing else.

She curled up into a ball in the back seat, still hearing the gun-fire, her body shaking. She was going to have an anxiety attack. No, no she couldn't. She had to make it home first.

At least she knew what was wrong with her. An Army doctor friend, while they were listening to enemy gunfire, and Sybil was shaking, said to her. "You know what's wrong with you?"

Sybil had shook her head, not hard with the rest of her shaking.

"You've got PTSD, girl. In med speak you're about to go over the edge."

Going over the edge sounded nice. Escaping all this, away, peaceful.

"Go home," her doctor friend said, "back to the womb. Stay there until you feel like coming out fighting." She doubled her fists, making boxing moves to emphasize her point.

Sybil thought about that night now in the back of the cab that seemed to be hurtling through space. She had taken her doctor friend's advice. She was going home, back to the womb. But the rat-a-tat of the gun was still in her head, vibrating her entire body.

She thought about the shooter. She only saw two thirds of his face, but he had a beatific look. The same look a suicide bomber she had seen had—maybe he was thinking of the thousand virgins waiting for him. The same smile before he blew himself up. She wasn't that close, but close enough to be peppered with sand and a piece of flesh on her face.

Her shaking was more violent.

Sweat.

"Are you okay, lady?"

"Yeah," she croaked. But she wasn't.

He had taken the direct route and landed her on Madison Avenue in Pasadena as she had requested.

Sybil stood on the walkway in front of the old Victorian house that had been her grandmother's. Now hers. Her grandmother had kept it up but Sybil knew that it had a hungry maw only money could feed. Her grandmother had left a sizeable 'upkeep' fund, in addition to what she had left Sybil.

It was not Sybil's dream house—but it was *hers*. That's all that mattered now. And it was her womb, where she had grown up. She pushed aside the thoughts of the last twenty-four hours, especially the last few.

Sybil climbed the steps to the veranda and rang the bell. Millie, her grandmother's housekeeper answered it immediately. "Welcome home. I'll make tea and a sandwich for you. Come down when you're ready." Millie bustled back down the hall to the kitchen. Sybil started for the stairs, thought about her room and the soft, comfortable bed. She shook her head, pulled off the backpack and left her carry-on at the foot the stairs. Then she went to the kitchen. Millie was always chirpy and cheery.

"I'd better not go upstairs and see that bed. Haven't slept for ages. Ah." Sybil sighed the last as Millie set down the teapot on a trivet in front of her usual place at the table. Sybil dropped to the chair. Real tea-leaf tea, real teapot, real china cup and saucer and a matching pitcher of real milk. She poured and drank and poured and drank, mentally, and maybe vocally, moaning in ecstasy.

Millie set a sandwich in front of her. Soft, white homemade bread. Tuna salad with bits of onion and celery for crunchiness, and lots of mayonnaise. Nothing had ever tasted so good. She chewed, extracting every flavor from the sandwich. Then downed another cup of tea.

"Thanks, Millie, you're the best."

Millie nodded as she wiped the counter, cleaning up the kitchen. Sybil knew Millie was only staying a month until she, Sybil, got settled, and then she was going to retire. It was time.

Sybil showered and washed her hair twice. All she could think of was bits of blood and flesh in her hair from the shooting. But that wasn't possible. Those hit were on the other side of the room where the shooter had been looking. Her hair was short so it dried quickly. It was easy care, but she always said she had to get her hair done when there was an assignment she didn't want to take. That became a running joke with her colleagues, even those with buzz cuts and very short haircuts, as most of the journalists and photographers had. No time and no place to get your hair done out there in the battlefields where she had spent the last few years.

Then she tumbled onto the soft mattress, clean sheets, fluffy comforter and that was it.

She slept for eighteen hours and woke to the aroma of bacon. She pulled on a robe, tied the sash tightly, then went downstairs.

As soon as she sat at the kitchen table, Millie set down a pot of tea on the trivet in front of her.

All of sudden Sybil remembered about her scheduled ride. How had she forgotten?

"What happened to Walt?"

Walt was a driver her grandmother had called whenever she wanted to go someplace, and for airport runs that Sybil did.

"Flat tire. He said he called you on your phone. You didn't get the message? He called after you had gone to bed to find out if you made it back okay. There was a shooting at the airport. Did you know about that?"

Sybil realized she had opened a can of worms with her question. The message was probably on her phone, which she hadn't even looked at in her haste to get away—as far away as she could and as fast as she could. She felt the silence from Millie. Why hadn't she, Sybil, known about Walt's call? *Please don't ask.* Sybil sent a mental message to Millie.

"Haven't checked my phone. Should have known it was something. He's so good about being on time."

"The shooting at the airport, he said he probably wouldn't have been able to get near your terminal."

"Shooting? I'll have to check it out." Just then the kitchen phone rang. "Carrington residence," Millie said. Then a moment later, "Who is calling, please?" another moment. "I'll see if she's in."

Sybil almost laughed at the grand lady façade. Millie covered the mouthpiece and said quietly, "Frank?"

Sybil nodded and took the phone, "Hi, Frank."

The voice from the other end said, "I've called you four times. Don't you answer your phone?"

"I was asleep. Just got up. What's happening?"

"What's happening is a shooting at the airport when you were probably there. I want you to go back and get the story."

"I quit, remember? I'm not going anywhere to get any story."

"Sybil, I love you, babe, get your ass out to the airport. Now."

"Frank, I love you, too, but my ass is not going to the airport." She saw Millie flinch. Her grandmother would definitely not approve of her language.

"You've got to get the story. You're sitting on top of it. Go."

"Frank, I quit. How many times do I have to quit? I'm burned out. I'm tired of being shot at. I want to sleep for at least a week." They talked for a few more minutes. Frank finally got the message and told her to take care of herself and he'd be back in touch.

Clicking off the phone at the same moment Millie set down a platter covered with a Denver omelet. The bacon aroma almost sent Sybil into a faint. Pieces of green pepper, Bermuda onion, mixed with the bacon and covered with cheese. In addition was a small dish of Millie's homemade catsup. A forkful of omelet dragged through the catsup was like mainlining heroin. Not that she knew about the latter, but she could envision the sensation. After devouring that and trying to savor each mouthful, she had the last cup of tea.

Then she dashed up to her room and checked her phone. Yes, Walt had called, and then the calls from Frank. She looked up the news on the shooting. The number killed and those hospitalized was listed but no names 'as the next of kin hasn't been informed.' Sybil noted with considerable interest that there was a quote from the FBI. Why were they involved? That was definitely intriguing and she felt a little tremor of hopping back into the fray. But it was only a *little* tremor. The *Los Angeles Times* would be on it, covering it from every angle. She didn't feel that need to be slogging through that field.

The thought of slogging brought her back to the muddy clothes she had in her backpack and carry-on. Both of the luggage pieces should be just thrown into the washer intact—or thrown out.

She went downstairs again. The best she could do at the moment was pull out her laptop and set it up in the kitchen. That would be her office for now. She'd be spending a lot of time in there.

When she went into the kitchen, Millie had left, but would be back to make her dinner and do whatever housecleaning was on the agenda. Lunch was probably a sandwich in the refrigerator and something yummy for dessert. Her bone-deep exhaustion had faded, but she still felt tired. She decided to walk around the neighborhood, get some fresh air that was free of the smoke of exploding bombs.

Walking around, she looked at the flowers, trees, grass, hedges, and the difference in each of the front yards of the houses on the neighboring streets. Individuality and old money showed. It was a little pocket of Pasadena that hadn't changed much.

Back to her laptop on the kitchen table, Sybil checked out the airport shooting story. Not much had been added. A few names which she looked up on the internet as the articles didn't give the background of the person, and wouldn't unless they were famous. None were. Another mention of the FBI.

In the days that followed, the reporting of the shooting shrunk, until finally there was no mention of it at all. Truly strange. No, she wasn't going to delve into it. Let others do that. She was tired of chasing around, tired of adrenaline surges, and tired of the aftermath. Just plain tired of being tired.

But the FBI was involved. Icy fingers in her stomach. Not good. If they found…found out she was a witness to the shooter's action, she'd be in deep trouble. And if Frank found out—

She assessed her situation. It had been simmering in the back of her head like a storm cloud, getting bigger and bigger. She had to face it, even though she didn't want to. She just wanted to hide in her house womb.

1) Frank would fire her for sure. She'd been a witness to a major story and hadn't written it, but rather ran from it. In Frank's eyes, they'd been scooped by another agency. Both were major crimes in the journalism world.

2) Frank would make sure she never worked in this town again. Never
    worked in the journalism field again—ever. He'd be sure everyone
    knew of her unprofessional act. She couldn't be relied on blahblah-
    blah. She'd be finished, never to work again as a trusted reporter.

Never to work again didn't sound all that bad at the moment. But
what was bad but what the FBI could do to her. That was worse.

Like other journalists working in war zones, the FBI relied on
them in part for domestic terrorist information. Journalists heard rumors,
gossip and had leads on possible attacks inside the US. Intel, it was
called. The journalists were handpicked and given what they called a 'get
out of jail card' as the FBI had promised to rescue them no matter who
captured them or where they were.

What she had just seen could be domestic terrorism. Yet she
hadn't told anyone. Not that she had a lot to tell the FBI, but the point
was she hadn't said anything. A big no-no. That meant she couldn't be
trusted by them either. And they'd make that known. Her 'get out of jail
card' would be turned over and the back of it would read *Go to Jail. Do
not pass Go. Do not collect $200.* As a journalist she had certain obliga-
tions and she'd just blown them all to hell. PSTD didn't cover her sins,
omissions and crimes. The FBI's retaliation for her actions—non-actions
actually. And when Frank fired her and sullied her reputation she'd be of
no value to the FBI.

She was not in any shape—physically or mentally— to be ha-
rassed by the FBI. They would want to know every scintilla of information about that encounter. They'd ask over and over again. The thought
of it all starting her shaking again. She didn't want that contact with the
FBI. She had to stay out of it. Her sanity depended on it.

Frank called again on the landline. Her phone was still sitting on
the dresser in her bedroom. A sure sign of her fragile state. She picked up
the handset in the kitchen.

"Hi, Sybil, how are you doing?"

"Hanging in there, Frank." Normally she would ask 'what's up?'
or 'what's my next assignment'—but not now.

A pause while he waited for those magic words, but when they didn't come he went on. "Keeping up on the airport shooting?"

"Yeah. An anomaly. An FBI spokesman made a comment. You probably caught that. What are they doing in this mix?"

"Good question, Sybil." He paused, probably waiting for her words of assent. Silence on her end so he said, "Love to have you answer that question with an article. Don't know who else I can send."

She clenched her jaw shut. If she mentioned names, he would say where each one was on assignment—war-torn Beirut, darkest, deep Africa, wherever. Which meant the only person left was her. There was a long silence on the line. She knew he was waiting for her to say something, to give in to his demands.

"You're sure you didn't find out anything? You were there at the same time."

"Frank, I was in *Arrivals*. The shooting took place in *Departures*."

Another pause. "The FBI angle is very interesting." He was trying to entice her, she knew. It was a very interesting angle, but mind and body couldn't get revved up enough to pursue it. "What if you—"

"No, no, no, no, and no."

"I get it. Your answer is no. Okay, call me when you want to talk, I won't bother you anymore." She knew that was pure fluff coming from him. He was relentless, which was what made him a great editor. "Take care, Sybil."

"You, too, Frank." She put the handset back in its cradle. Then she filled the kettle, turned on the gas, put a spoonful of tea leaves in the teapot, found her favorite cup and saucer set. She had to get an electric kettle. Her grandmother never wanted one. Thought something about it was unsanitary, or that the water didn't taste the same, whatever. Sybil wanted one. But even a trek to the store seemed beyond her. She put it on the grocery list—that was a step forward.

Drinking the tea, she leaned against the stove thinking about the shooting. She could have done something. She realized she was considering action after having several days of rest. At the time she was almost catatonic with lack of sleep and jetlag. Not to mention PTSD. Plus if she had rushed forward, she would have had to slip off her heavy backpack. She wouldn't have been able to reach him in time. She was strong, but not stronger than him in her depleted condition. He was a man with a mission and was going to accomplish that. Did he accomplish his mission? What was it?

She poured more tea and milk into the delicate cup. Those were all questions she would have asked if she wasn't so burned out. She knew she wouldn't be able to get rid of all of her journalistic instincts forever, but for right now, they were at a low level.

Frank called two days later. She was sitting at her laptop on the kitchen table, having her 'elevenses' a joke about tea at 11 a.m. "How are you holding up, Sybil?"

"Fine, Frank." She said nothing more. Let him to do the talking.

"I got one of the stringers to bulldog the airport shooting story."

"Hey, Frank, that's great." Sybil was enthusiastic that someone else had the job.

"Wonder if she could touch base with you on a few journalistic points."

"She can't write?"

"Yeah, yeah, but I want you to add the professional touch."

Sybil felt she was being sucked into the story—exactly what she didn't want. On the other hand she wasn't getting any information from the internet so maybe this was her way of keeping up with the story. She weighed both options, knowing how Frank operated. "I'm going on vacation so I can only do email and phone."

"Where are you going?" The question alerted her to the fact that Frank was being devious and hoped she'd go out on an assignment.

"Veranda Bay. Very quiet, hasn't been discovered by tourists yet. Has all the comforts of home." She heard his keyboard clicking and swallowed a laugh.

"Long Island? Antigua?" Surprise sent his voice went up a couple of notches.

"No. California. As I said it's not on the tourist map yet."

"Okay, email and phone." Resignation in his voice. A few moments of silence while he readjusted his goals, she thought. "How long?"

"Two weeks, at least, maybe longer if I like the place."

"Two weeks?" More resignation. The LAX shooting would be old news by then, immediacy having lost its edge. "Are you sure you weren't there, at the airport, saw the shooting?"

Icy fingers on her neck. *He couldn't possibly know. Couldn't possibly.* But he did have an uncanny instinct in being able to read his journalists' voices, as most of the time that's all he had to go on—taking their temperature. *Had she revealed something?* "You're kicking a dead horse, Frank." That was her grandmother's favorite saying. As a little girl she analyzed the words and never understood fully what it meant, but she knew what her grandmother meant in answer to her plea for something— again.

"Just seems so right. You're a magnet. You're always in the right place at the right time. You had to be there, you had to see everything. I just know it."

"Wishful thinking." She had to say little, be careful of what she said. He'd pick up for sure what the truth was.

"Okay, I'll give her your email and phone number. I've told her to look into the FBI angle. There's a story there, like you said. Anything else?"

"There's only been two obits. Five people died. Where are the other obits? Might not be any, but I think it's worth looking into. Feet on the ground, not fingers on the keyboard, and the latter's all I'm doing. As I said I'm going on vacation. You might admit I deserve one."

"Yeah, yeah, okay. Take a vacation, leave me high and dry with a stringer."

Sybil laughed. A real laugh this time. He was so funny, this act of being pathetic. He wasn't. It was just one of the tools in his box. "I'll have a drink for you at Verandah Bay."

Some sound like *humph* before he disconnected.

Sybil got up, stretched and went out the front door, closing the screen behind her. Then she laughed again and spread out her arms. *Verandah Bay*. With white wicker furniture, and a pitcher of lemonade— her grandmother's favorite. Sybil liked the passion fruit drinks Millie made for her, while she and grandmother sat on Verandah Bay.

But Sybil didn't find the peace there that she had had with her grandmother who always sat in the rocker on the other side of the small table that held the tray with pitchers of lemonade and passion fruit. She was uneasy, not at rest, and analyzed what was bothering her. She realized it was the shooting at the airport and her proximately to it. And the fact that she'd scuttled out. 'Fessing up to the FBI would not make her feel any better. In fact it would make her feel worse—questioning over and over, being looked at as some sort of participant, in essence, looking guilty. She had to make a decision, get the guilt off her mind, or 'fess up. She thought long and hard about it. If her grandmother had been sitting there, Sybil wasn't sure she would even talk about it to her. The decision maker was that she couldn't handle any more stress, so she shoved her misgivings into a box in her head. The box was overstuffed and hard to close.

Her phone vibrated. Ann Simpson, Frank's stringer. After a few 'hi-how-are-you-type stuff, Ann summarized what she had so far. Hardly a hair's info over what the *Los Angeles Times* had reported. Ann listed all the sources she had contacted—the usual 'suspects'—LAPD, airport PR, and so on. Protocol, right on target, and by the book.

"The FBI's not forthcoming at all?" Sybil asked.

"On-going case rigmarole."

They talked about a few other leads, all standard, but Ann said she was dead-ended.

"Here are a couple of thoughts. Talk with the reporter from the *Los Angeles Times*, find out why they aren't carrying the story anymore. Hang around in that terminal and talk with some of the workers—custodians, ticket agents, anybody who works there."

"Okay, got it. What else?"

"What about the TSA people?"

"They've all been moved to another terminal. There's a whole new crew."

Sybil mulled that over. "Then go to the other terminal. See if you can catch any of them on their break. They're traumatized, they're ripe to talk. Plus they've been abandoned, it sounds like, after they've given their witness' statements. They're needy, get to them. Also there are only two obits, see if you can find out the names of the others and get their obits."

"'Haven't notified next of kin' is the answer I get."

"You gotta find out why the FBI is involved. That's the key to everything. Something big was going on. I know you've tried. Next item is the gun. An antique. You said you were able to talk to the collector?"

"Yeah, he didn't know it was missing until the FBI and ATF showed up at his door with the gun. He checked his locked cabinet. Not there. Then he checked where he keeps the ammunition in a separate locked cabinet in another room. That was missing, too."

"Go with that angle. Was he on vacation for a while? Who has access to his place? The guy who used the gun either got in somehow, or he had someone else get it for him. How's ATF? Are they clamming up, too?"

"No, they're very good about giving me info. The collector is very open, baffled, and trying to figure out what happened. He's got a special permit to collect and sell antique machine guns. I've checked him out. He's on the up-and-up. There'd be no reason for him to sell, he likes these guns too much."

"Does he use them, go out shooting, target practice? Anything like that?"

"I'll check with him on that, and the access. There's one more thing. The FBI is checking up on the people who left the terminal after the shooting."

Icy fingers crawled around in Sybil's torso again. She clutched it with one hand trying to quell their movement. "What people?"

"The ones who had checked in, had boarding passes, but left when the shooting happened."

"They just took off?"

"Yep. I would, too."

I did. "Any names, can you interview them?"

"Working on it," Ann said, "But I doubt I'll get anywhere."

"What about the ones in the hospital. Anybody on the critical list? Can you get in to talk to any of them?"

"Yeah, I'm checking out the hospital. FBI put a clamp on that. I'm trying to get in to talk to them."

"Good work, Ann. I don't have any other thoughts. Except I think the TSA people might be a goldmine. They're probably been told not to talk, but I think they will. Someone will. Might check to see if anyone's quit. They'd be perfect."

"Okay, thanks. You've got my number now, and I'll send you an email so you'll have my addy."

They signed off. Sybil wondered if the FBI could find her. If someone had noticed her and looked at her luggage tags on her backpack and carry-on— She'd have to cross that bridge when it loomed up. It was possible. Let them come to her, she wasn't going to them. Although it might be a great way to get some info. But she wasn't that desperate. She wasn't writing the story.

Sybil had another thought for Ann to check out. Then the ramifications of that hit her. Cameras in the airport. She would be on it. They wouldn't find her name as someone who had a boarding pass. So they'd start looking at cameras in other parts of the airport. They'd find her. Check out who had left the plane. And find her.

TWO MONTHS LATER

Sybil saw them coming up the walkway. The woman looked familiar. The guy—he could only be a cop even though he wasn't in uniform. As they approached the screen door, Sybil realized he was wearing a uniform of sorts—a suit.

"Sybil? Hi. It's me, Ann Simpson." Ah that's why she looked familiar. She'd seen her pix on emails. She knew they could see her through the screen. She looked at the man.

"Sybil Carrington? I'm Eli Walsh, FBI."

~The End~

THE SUITCASE

A shooting at LAX has affected the lives of several women. This is one of the stories. Trudy's suitcase was tampered with—which involved her in the shooter's actions. And through this and the other stories we learn more about the shooter.

Trudy's phone chimed. "Blair?"

"I parked the car, can't get into the terminal. Somebody says there's been a shooting. Are you all right?" Blair's voice was shrill.

"Yeah, that's what I heard too. A shooting somewhere here. I didn't see anything or hear anything. I'm still waiting for my suitcase. There's a long line to go through the final passport check, but they're not letting anyone out."

"Okay, I'll go back to the car and wait. Call me when you're coming out."

"Thanks. Babies are crying all over the place. I feel like joining them. Maybe throwing a tantrum."

"Won't do you any good. I'm here for you."

Trudy sighed. *Where is my suitcase?* At least she'd have a ride home from her colleague and temporary housemate. No shuttle that circled the airport three times looking for more customers. And no cab driver needed. All the ones she'd ever had drove like a bat with singed wings flying out of hell. They were always trying to get back to the airport to pick up another fare. Uber or Lyft were plan B.

Trudy thought about all the years she'd flown out of here. LAX was always under construction or renovation or 'pardon our dust.' It was always so confusing to know where to go. She hated it. But what was the alternative—maybe a private jet. *Dream on!*

"Trudy Soames?"

Trudy nodded. A man and a woman in suits. Government something.

"Would you come with us and identify your suitcase? There seems to be some mix-up with the luggage tags." The man spoke.

Why didn't she believe him? *Maybe because she'd spent the last twenty years with liars of one sort or another.*

"I wondered what happened to it. Everyone else from my plane got their luggage."

They ushered her into an office in the baggage claim area. No window. There, a suitcase sat. At first glance she didn't think it was hers. No red wool tie on the handle. And stickers on it. Not hers.

"Please sit for a moment, we have a couple of questions to ask you about your suitcase." The woman talked this time.

Then Trudy saw the luggage tag. *That* was hers. She reached for it, but the man pushed it out of her grasp. Trudy sat back, miffed about being held up like this, plus so tired after the long flight, but resigned that she wasn't going to be getting out as quickly as she thought.

The woman took a picture out of a file folder. Trudy realized she had been carrying a clipboard. "Can you tell us about this picture?"

Trudy looked at the picture. The person in it sort of looked like her, wore an orange muumuu, and had her arm around the shoulder of a man in his 20s.

"That's not me," she said. "I don't have an orange dress like that. I do know who the man is and I would not be putting my arm around him. Let alone posing for a picture with him."

The woman was still standing, didn't say anything for a few seconds. The man stood beside the suitcase. "It looks like you," the woman finally said.

"It's not me."

The man laid the suitcase flat and snapped it open. On the top was the orange muumuu the woman wore in the picture.

Trudy gaped. "That's not mine. What's under it?" The man lifted the outfit. She noticed that he wore latex gloves. A red blouse and other things she recognized. "Those are mine. What's under it, not the top thing. Where's my Harrod's bag? I bought some presents and crammed them into my suitcase. I could barely close it."

The woman said, "You're saying the dress is not yours?"

"Yes," Trudy answered, "It is not mine. and I never saw it before, nor did I ever wear it for a picture." She spaced out her words as though she was talking to a two-year-old. Then realized there was no point in getting huffy. They were just doing their job. She'd been there, done that.

Trying to soften her stance, she went on. "How did that get in there? Since we can't lock it, I guess anyone could open it."

"Excuse us a moment." The woman and the man stepped out and closed the door. Trudy looked around. Nothing in the room besides two metal chairs with cracked brown fake leather seat and back, and a small metal table with a scratched grey top. No memos or signs on the wall. Sterile. She recognized it as an interview room. She was afraid she would be claustrophobic any minute. She closed her eyes. Then she thought about Blair. She tried to call her, but Trudy's phone showed *No Service*.

Trudy stood up, a little shaky, and went to the door, only three steps—the room seemed to be getting smaller. She turned the knob. No surprise, the door didn't open. Locked. She took some deep breaths, fighting panic. A moment later the door opened, and the two came back in.

"I have to call my friend, she's here to pick me up. She'll wonder what happened," Trudy said.

"Just a few more minutes and then we'll get you past the line out there." The woman gestured to her to sit down again. The woman sat this time, then asked if she could record their conversation. Trudy said 'yes', then they went over again everything that Trudy had said.

"Tell me about the man in the picture," the woman asked.

"I will, but tell me first what's this all about?" Trudy asked.

The woman seemed to be in considerable thought. The man stood behind Trudy so she didn't know what he was doing. When the woman looked up at him. Trudy turned around and saw him nodding, apparently giving her the okay.

"There's been a shooting here in the airport. We have the shooter neutralized. He had this picture on him. Just before the shooting we received a tip describing you and your suitcase. The tip was that there was some evidence in the suitcase that we would be interested in and related to the shooting. At this moment that's all we know."

The woman seemed drained of all information. Trudy believed her.

Trudy took a deep breath. *Where to start?* "As you probably know I'm an ADA, Assistant District Attorney for L. A. County." She pointed to the picture. "He was arrested for attempted theft. He tried to steal a gun." Then she stopped. "Is he the shooter?"

"Please continue," the woman said.

Ohhkaay. "His ID was a driver's license, so he was booked under that name, but when they scanned his prints, it came back with a different name. LAPD, they were the arresting police officers, had to sort that out." She tried to summarize the complicated case with mixed identities.

"You were the A.D.A. on the case?

Trudy nodded. "LAPD dropped all charges, so he was free to go."

"That wasn't the end of it?" the woman said.

"Obviously not," Trudy said, looking at the picture.

"Did he threaten you?"

Trudy thought for a moment. "Not that I know of. But I had to leave the case and someone else did the paperwork. I went on medical leave. Then I decided to take a vacation, which I haven't done for a long time."

She could feel them wanting to ask what her medical condition was, and it almost made her laugh. Then again, maybe they knew. They were all silent for a few minutes.

"We'll come to your house in about a week with your suitcase," the man said. He almost said it as a question, as though asking her permission. She nodded.

They ushered her out, bypassing the long line and the passport control officers who were checking everyone's picture and passport—again. It had been done once by machine, and then by an officer. Trudy felt they were looking for someone. And well they should if there was a shooting here. Outside the building she called Blair, and within a few minutes she saw her across the street and waved. Trudy looked at the two agents and they nodded. She walked across the street between the terminal and the parking structure and hugged Blair. She knew if she started crying, she'd never stop. She choked out to Blair, "I'll tell you later."

Blair took her arm and led her to the car. "I'm going to have a hellava parking charge. Are you okay?"

Trudy could only nod. She was tired, dehydrated and needed something to eat. Light at the end of the tunnel—was home.

That night Trudy lay awake reliving the scene with the two agents. FBI they'd told her. She didn't ask for ID. A tip, they had said, about her suitcase. Where did the orange muumuu come from? No question that between the time she dropped her suitcase off at the check-in counter in London to the time she saw it, anyone could have opened it. How many people had access to it between London and Los Angeles? Even in the days when you could lock your suitcase people could get into it.

And where was her Harrod's bag. Who stole that?

She relived the scene over and over until it finally wore her out and she fell asleep into a vigorous dream. She was being chased by a plane in a field like Cary Grant in *North by Northwest*. Nowhere to escape to. When she jerked awake, she could hear Blair in the other room lightly snoring. Good for her. At least one of them was sleeping soundly and would be alert the next day. It was already the next day but too early to get up, so she lay exhausted after her energetic dream.

In a week, the two appeared at the door of her home in Arcadia. Blair had gone to work—she was an A.D.A. also.

The man held up her Harrod's bag. Trudy was jubilant. "You've found it! Come on in. Coffee?"

They sat in the living room, the two on chairs in front of the coffee table and Trudy on the other side on the sofa looking through the Harrod's bag. "Everything seems to be here. How did you find it?"

"It was stuffed behind a trash container in the baggage area."

Trudy went over the possibilities. "The muumuu was put in my suitcase there?"

The man was doing most of the talking this time. "Analysis shows that the dress was thoroughly washed, so no DNA, and that it had not been on the plane. We viewed the video from the baggage area about the time the shooting occurred. It couldn't have been the shooter because your plane landed just minutes after he was taken down. We'll show you the video. See if you can identify the person."

The woman pulled a laptop out of her briefcase and set it up on the coffee table, then started the video.

In the video a man was standing right by the chute where the suitcases spilled out onto the conveyer belt. He grabbed one, pulled off the red wool tie, plastered some stickers on the suitcase—all actions done quickly, almost in the blink of an eye.

He then pulled the suitcase behind the unused adjoining carrel. He opened the suitcase took out a Harrod's bag and put something into the suitcase, closed it and rolled it back to the original conveyer belt. Then he walked over to a trash container and dropped the Harrod's bag behind it. He strode out of sight.

"No wonder I couldn't find my suitcase," Trudy said.

"Our lab says the picture was doctored. Your face over whoever had an arm about him."

Trudy nodded. "Had to be something like that. He must have thought it was funny to show me with my arm around him like we were buddy buddy. I had a strong aversion to him the first time I met him. Psychopath. Sociopath. Take your pick. Did not want to handle that case."

"Apparently he took a liking to you," the woman said with a smile.

Trudy laughed.

"Next up is trying to ID his accomplice in this video. Do you recognize him?" the man asked.

Trudy shook her head.

"The tip we received about a suitcase described it with stickers. We knew what to look for. You can imagine how we jumped on that. But when we checked you out, nothing added up especially after we talked to you. Then we saw the video. When we listened again to the recording of the tip, it all sounded a little too pat. How could you be involved when you just landed? As I said, nothing added up."

"Thanks for not cuffing and locking me up. Hard to explain that to the D.A. I'm told you already talked to her."

The man nodded. "And to the Public Defender who handled the case. He says much the same as you did. He had 'bad vibes' from his client."

"Bad vibes sums it up. Why did the accomplice carry through with his mission when his friend, the shooter, was dead?"

"Don't have an answer to that question. Let's play the video again. Double check if you recognize him."

Trudy leaned closer to the laptop screen, trying to see the man's face, but the high angle of the camera and the baseball cap hit the top half of his face and hair.

"Same answer as before. I don't know who he is. None of the shooter's friends match up?"

"Friends? He was a loner," the man said. "No thoughts about who else might want to incriminate you?"

Trudy shrugged. "Anybody getting out of prison that I helped put there. Can't think of anyone specifically."

They both slightly nodded. To Trudy that meant it tallied with what they already knew.

Trudy asked, "How did the accomplice get into the baggage area? That's only for the passengers."

"We're looking into that. It might give us a lead. But we don't know yet."

They talked for a few more minutes, drinking another mug of coffee. Trudy asked about the shooter, could they tell her about the person, but they declined. Time for them to leave. Trudy knew she hadn't seen the last of them. At the door the woman said, "Be careful, he's still out there."

Trudy nodded. She didn't know if the accomplice was carrying out the shooter's revenge, but why would he? Or if he had his own revenge on her.

The shooting at the airport case was in the D.A.'s jurisdiction.

But it looked like the FBI was involved and probably the ATF, Homeland Security, the Airport Police, and a bunch of other agencies. If it had been the D.A.'s case she would be able to find out a lot more information. She probably still could. The more she thought about it, the more her ulcer started to bother her. An inner open wound that her body squirted acid onto. That was what it felt like—and that was the reason for her medical leave. Such a mundane problem that incapacitated her.

Time to think of other things.

She cooked dinner, something she rarely had time or the inclination to do when she was working full time. When Blair came home from the D.A.'s office, they had a good conversation while eating and sharing a bottle of wine. The tart taste of the chianti was so good with the chunky tomato sauce and juicy veal-and-beef meatballs over fettucine.

Blair told her about the happenings at the office, some wild, some sad. And that was just the staff. Trudy asked about the shooter but Blair said there was little information about him, as the FBI was holding its cards close to its bullet-proof vest. "S.O.P." said Trudy. Blair nodded. *Standard Operating Procedure.*

"What's happening with your ex-to-be? Is he still harassing you?"

Blair shook her head. "All quiet on the western front," she said. "Nothing further since he tried to break in here."

While Trudy was away on vacation and Blair was asleep, the burglar alarm went off. It echoed in the cul-de-sac so that all the neighbors turned on lights, peered out to see what was happening. The kitchen window had been cracked but not broken. Blair was able to see the man run off. And recognized who he was.

When Trudy had been viewing the video on the baggage claim area she tried to match up the figure with Blair's ex-to-be, definitely not a nice guy, but it wasn't him. She wished it had been so they could stash him in jail for a while.

"Haven't heard a peep out of him."

"But you're apprehensive."

"Feel a lot better now that you're back," Blair said.

They both had guns. And they both qualified on their weapons. Trudy had had hers for a while, reluctant, but she'd had threats and other ADAs carried, so Trudy finally gave up her resistance and went along with the tide. Blair had only been an ADA for five years and had to be convinced that she should have a weapon also. She, too, finally bought one.

"I hope he tries again," Blair said. "I'll be ready for him next time."

"No, you'll be ready for the intruder who tries to break in. You don't know who it is." Trudy gave her a stern look

"Whoops. I'll let you have the honors." They didn't laugh. Trudy was worried that he *would* try again. But then she had her own worry— the man who tampered with her suitcase. Would he try to do something else to her, since the suitcase caper didn't work?

In the morning Trudy stood in the living room with her coffee, looking out at the street. She was a nodding acquaintance with all of the residents in Maiden Lane. The first house had only a side window facing the cul-de-sac, the front of it was the cross street. Trudy considered that it was unoccupied. Lights came on at the same time every day, so she guessed they were on a timer. Gardeners appeared every week, but she never saw anyone else. The house next to it that did face Maiden Lane was owned by a lieutenant in the Sheriff's Department, and his wife. Next to them was a CPA and wife, then a couple who were professors at Cal Tech, then a judge and his son, a school principal and her sister, and a bank official. Trudy's house was next and on the other side of her was a retired couple, maybe in their 90s, whom she rarely saw. They had a high fence around their backyard, with one rose bush that draped over the white wood slats. Every year it was trimmed back and then grew even more prolific. They had the lot next to them that was a mini forest. The last house on her side faced the cross street.

Trudy always thought about having a block party, maybe on the Fourth of July, but never did anything about it. That was the extent of her neighborliness—the thought of it. But that was then, and this was now. She'd do it!

Trudy considered contacting, or walking across the street to the Lieutenant. She hadn't talked to Blair about this, but she decided she wasn't going to do anything right now.

Except—there he was, walking toward her front door. Smitson, that was his name. He rang the bell and she opened the door. He was at least 6'5" and whatever workout program he had he was sticking to it religiously. Not in uniform, khakis and white polo shirt with the badge emblem on it.

"Hi, Miss Soames. I'd like to talk with you for a few minutes.

"Come on in. Coffee? Let's talk in the kitchen."

They sat at the table next to the cracked window. Blair had offered to get it fixed, but Trudy had said to leave it for now—to remind them to be vigilant. Trudy made sure the burglar alarm still worked perfectly. And she'd had motion lights installed. Not going to work every day meant she had the time for all the things she thought about doing and never got around to.

"I wanted to let the two of you know that I've got a stalker. So far he doesn't have my address, but I'm sure he'll get it somehow. If you see any strange cars or people wandering around call the police. Arcadia P.D.is going to do some extra patrols here—"

Trudy laughed before he finished, and even more when she saw the quick array of expressions flash over his face. They went from surprised to *'ohmygod, a loony'*.

"Let me tell you about our threats." She told him about the suitcase episode at LAX, and how the cracked window came to be. She pointed to it and said, "Our souvenir."

"I was here the night the alarm went off. Didn't see anybody, but I was ready with my weapon. Any more encounters?"

Trudy shook her head.

"The judge, too, says he's been threatened, but it's happened so many times, he doesn't pay any attention. Do you have a weapon?"

"We both do." Then she told him she was on medical leave so would be around more than usual.

"Nice to know I'm in good threatened company," he said, with a smile. "They've transferred me to administration for now," he said as if to explain his clothes. "They're going to keep me there until the threat dies down." He pulled out his phone. "Let's exchange numbers."

When Blair came home, Trudy told her what her thought had been about letting Smitson know of the threats—and then how he had appeared with his own threat hanging over his head.

A bottle of wine with the dinner Trudy had cooked—chunky sauce over fettucine with spicy sausage—made the many threats in their small cul-de-sac seem almost amusing. Almost.

The same two FBI Agents came back again to show her another video. This time is was of the man who had tampered with her suitcase.

"How did you find him?" Trudy asked.

The man answered. "We followed him by way of the cameras outside the terminal and in the parking structure. Lucky for us he had parked there. We got his license plate number as he drove off, traced him to his address. Arrested him. Piece of cake."

"Devil's Food," Trudy said.

The woman laughed, but it took the man a moment to make the connection. "Very good."

"I don't have cake, but I have some cookies. I'll get coffee."

A few minutes later, the video was running. It was taken in an interview room with the woman asking the questions. The arrestee had one hand handcuffed to the chair, but that didn't stop him from trying to gesture with both hands.

"Here's the salient part," the woman said.

We have you on video in the baggage area, taking one of the suitcases. Why did you do that?

This guy, met him at a hop shop—

A marijuana store?

Yeah, yeah, a hop shop. We get to talking and then we go out for beer. He's buying, so I'm listening. Says he wants to play a practical joke on his girlfriend who's just coming back from England. And wants to know if I'd do something for him and he'd pay me. So I ask him how much and he says a Cleveland.

A thousand dollars?

Yeah, yeah, but I didn't know that at the time. I didn't know what a Cleveland was, except the city. Even the banks don't know what it is.

He gave you the bill?

He showed it to me. Says it was worth a lot more because it was in mint condition and the bills had been discontinued. He said to go on eBay and check the sale price. I got this girlfriend and she works in a bank so I asked her about it. She said he was right, but I probably wouldn't be able to get smaller bills for it at a bank. She said she'd find out, then I never heard from her no more.

You took the bill?

Yeah, yeah, didn't I just say that? Then he told me what he wanted me to do. Seemed like nothing, so I said I'd do it. I don't know nothing about any shooting. I didn't know he was going to shoot the place up. I swear I knew from nothing about that. He was a little weird. Shoulda known it wasn't going to be easy. Next thing I know is I got the whole FBI surrounding my house. Oh, man, that was scary.

The woman turned the video off. "What do you think?" the man asked.

Trudy kept staring at the screen as though she was still watching it. She was—in her mind. "I've dealt with a lot of liars in my time—but he's not one of them. He's telling the truth. Makes sense the shooter would get somebody on the fringes who could use the money. A marijuana shop was the perfect place to meet somebody like that. Was the bill counterfeit?"

"Nope. Good as gold," the man answered.

"I hope he gets to keep it, or gets smaller bills that he can actually use."

"We're going to take care of that. Thanks for your cooperation—and for the cookies and coffee." The man stood as the woman closed the laptop.

"I don't have to worry about anyone coming after me? Revenge or anything like that?"

"We don't know if there are any other accomplices. But it doesn't look like it." He looked at the woman, and she nodded.

"That's a big relief," Trudy said as she walked with them to the front door.

She called Smitson to update him on the arrest. "One down, two to go," she said and heard him laugh.

Over dinner, she said to Blair, "Nice guys. What good does that do the shooter after he's dead? To have me implicated in something." She waved her hand as though to dissipate the question out of the air. "I guess that's like asking why some guy shoots his family then himself. Why doesn't he commit suicide first?" Trudy shook her head.

"Have some more wine," Blair said in way of an answer. "Is it bothering your stomach at all?"

"I'm feeling a lot better now that the guy was caught. I didn't relish going over all my cases to see who just got released and might be, literally, gunning for me. If your question is when am I going to go back to work—my answer is I'm still thinking about it. This whole thing—the shooting at the airport has got me thinking about what life is about."

"Do you have an answer?"

Trudy laughed. "In *vino veritas*, but no, I don't have an answer. Isn't it enough I came up with the question?"

Trudy woke up. A noise. Outside. She rolled over and reached for the book with *The Bible* in gold letters on its spine that sat on the bottom shelf of her nightstand. She opened the cover—it was a box—and took out her gun. In the hall she checked that the safety was on so she wouldn't accidently shoot herself in the foot. She went out of her opened bedroom door into the hallway.

"Blair?" she whispered.

"I'm here. Got my gun."

"Me, too. What was it?"

"Somebody's at the side of the house in the bushes, now they've moved around front."

"The motion lights should have come on." She wondered about that. "I'm calling Smitson."

When he answered, she said, "We've got a prowler. Might have disabled the motion lights. Maybe the alarm, too."

'I'm on it. If you've got your weapons, don't shoot me by mistake."

Trudy would have laughed, but the possibility was there. "Roger that."

Moments later there was gunfire—and the motion lights came on.

Trudy peered out of the living room window. Two bodies lay on her front lawn amid the cactus plants.

She could see Smitson across the street but he wasn't in firing stance. Lights were coming on in the cul de sac and soon there was an Arcadia police car. Then two. Then three. Flashing lights all over. Smitson was on his phone, no gun in sight, but he did have his LASD jacket on.

"Blair, stash your gun." Trudy did the same. Then they stood by the front window, drapes parted slightly, watching the action.

"It's my ex," Blair said.

"Are you sure? Who's the other guy?"

"Yes, it's him. I hope he's dead."

Trudy thought how sad it was that one fell in love—but with a Jekyll and Hyde character—then later, was glad he was dead.

The other body turned out to be Smitson's stalker. Blair's ex and the stalker had shot each other. The stalker had the address in his pocket, but he had the last two digits reversed so it was Trudy's address, not

Smitson's. In the dark, he must have thought Blair's ex was Smitson and shot him. Blair's ex had a gun so it was a no-brainer what he planned to do with it.

The Coroner's van, then the Sheriff's lab techs, the interviews by Arcadia P.D. and LASD took up most of the night into the morning. Blair called her office and told them why she wasn't coming today.

Trudy made breakfast, while Blair kept them supplied with coffee. They rehashed the scene long after they'd eaten. Blair said she'd be going home now that her ex was no longer there. Trudy offered to go with her, see if they needed to hire a cleaning crew.

Then Blair asked her if she had thought more about what she was going to do—go back to the D.A.'s or not. They had some laughs about what Trudy could do if she didn't go back, such as gardener. She definitely needed to do a little replanting in her now-ruined cactus garden out front. Or maybe chef since she'd been getting a lot of practice lately. Then they made up a lot of funny professions Trudy could go into.

Trudy told Blair that her doctor has said her ulcer would only get better without stress. But if she went back to work, she'd have stress. So what was the answer?

Trudy knew what the answer was in her gut—right where the ulcer was. She wasn't going back. There had to be other positions in the law—because she loved the law and everything associated with it. She still loved her job, but she couldn't do it anymore. So criminal work was out. She didn't know what she wanted to do—but she did know what she *didn't* want to do.

The shooting at the airport had affected her and she hadn't even seen the action. But she'd been involved. One thing she wanted to do was find out more about the shooting and the shooter. There was little enough in the news for some reason.

Trudy sat at the kitchen table and decided what she was going to do. She gave her stomach the test and no acid squirted on her wound.

She was going to find out why someone paid the man to put the muumuu in her suitcase. How he knew her suitcase. Why he picked her out. Did she have a stalker? Someone with a vendetta?

Then she thought about the shooting. Was this a diversionary tactic? How could it be? Was someone trying to connect her to the shooting? Delay in some way?

Then she wondered if her suitcase had been mistaken for someone else's? That made more sense. Who was the other person? Or was the suitcase just taken at random? It was a plain black one that almost everyone had.

No matter, that was her mission. All she had to do was get more information from the FBI. Maybe she could be a consultant. She ran that by her ulcer. No reaction. Her ulcer was okay with her new plan.

~The End~

THE BULLET

Simone and her sister are both injured when the shooter randomly sprays the area with bullets. A life changing experience in more ways than one.

THE BULLET

Simone bent to pick up her carryon to put it in the lineup on the conveyor belt. "No," her sister said. "Let me do that. You have a weak heart."

Her sister hadn't mentioned her weak heart much, but they lived their life around it. Simone had been diagnosed by their old family doctor when she was eight—just after their parents had been killed in a car crash. Her sister was ten years older and had taken care of her ever since. Her sister believed in homeopathic remedies, grew her own medicinal plants, and made sure their diet was of healthy foods. Simone didn't think too often about her weak heart—it was just there.

At that moment she heard a loud noise, and her sister knocked against her and they both fell to the floor. Simone's head struck a metal stanchion. All she knew vaguely was that she felt so comfortable just lying there and didn't want to move—except her sister lay sprawled over her and something wet was soaking her blouse.

"Pulse's thready on this one. Gurney," yelled someone kneeling next to her.

Simone wanted to cover her ears, but she couldn't move. Then she felt a hand on her wrist. "This one's good," a woman said. A weight was lifted off her. She thought about the boy in a movie saying something like, "He's not heavy, Father. He's my brother." Only she was heavy even though she was her sister.

In the hospital near LAX, Simone found out that they'd been involved in a shooting at the airport. Five dead, maybe more, and several wounded. She was not wounded by a bullet, as the others were, but had concussion and a hairline crack in her skull. They were keeping her in for observation as she felt sleepy all the time—not good. What was good, the woman doctor told her, was that she didn't have a headache.

She asked about her sister's condition. The same doctor treated her and her sister, and some others who had been shot. The doctor said her sister was still in a coma and they didn't know when she'd come out of it. Simone inferred from the look on the doctor's face that the possibility of her breathing on her own was nil.

102

Simone stayed with her sister as much as she could. She sat in a chair holding her sister's hand, but kept dozing off. Sitting up and dozing was better than lying in bed and dozing. At least that's what she inferred from the hospital personnel who marched in and out of the room every few minutes.

Roaming around the hospital, she was able to be in contact with the other shooting victims, visiting and finding out what happened to them. Several uniformed and street-clothed members of various policing organizations kept up a round of interviews, and sometimes dropped a piece of information that Simone harvested.

The two topics of conversation whenever she visited—now a close-knit group of vicitms and their families—were their wounds, and the shooting at the airport.

At least they were all healing—Simone's sister was the only one not on the mend. The others were looking forward to their release—but her sister wasn't looking forward to anything. She stayed in a coma.

When Simone got back from her rounds she told her sister about the other patients and their families. She was so used to sharing every-thing with her sister that talking to her seemed to be the most natural thing for her to do, even though her sister's eyes were closed. What registered, no one knew.

One piece of information she didn't share with her sister—and she couldn't give herself a reason why—was that the doctor had told her she didn't have a weak heart or any sort of heart condition.

Simone had to mull that over. Would their lives have been dif-ferent if they had both known that? She felt now it had given her sister a purpose in life. No, she wouldn't tell her sister—she wanted her to live and think she had a reason to do so.

The sleepiness that Simone had constantly experienced was now gone. Her doctor told her she could be discharged. Simone moved into the nearby motel where family members of the other shooting patients were staying. Since she and her sister had both packed for a month's vacation, Simone had everything she needed for her stay.

Simone found herself becoming Information Central as she spent time with the hospital staff, the motel clerks, as well as the patients and their families.

Everyone was anxious to learn more about the shooting. They all tried to get information from the two FBI agents who were handling the case, but the two were not in the business of *giving* information. However, occasionally something slipped out. In the evenings the motel residents pooled the tidbits while having dinner in the adjoining restaurant.

By canvassing all of her sources—there was always someone who knew someone—she found a nurse whose brother lived next door to the antique machine gun collector. Jasmine, the nurse-sister, had to pry information from her brother as he wasn't all that interested. He had a new girlfriend and that was the focus of his life. No matter that law enforcement officials were visiting his neighbor so often that they made appointments so they wouldn't trip over each other.

On the motel's internet Simone researched antique machine guns, as that's what the shooter used. Here was a world she knew nothing about, but she also learned a lot more about the shooting. Just posted was an interview with a gun collector. Some of the patients had made guesses as to what the gun was that the shooter had used—Thompson, and some other names, but no one knew for sure.

The owner of the gun in question was a collector, restorer and repairer of most antique guns, but specialized in antique machine guns. The antique guns had to be deactivated, meaning they could not be fired. Even though they couldn't be fired, they could be restored. He had three on his workbench that were in different stages of repair. One of those was missing. The FBI had found it—in the hands of the shooter.

The collector owned a three-bedroom ranch house-style house. He lived in the master bedroom, bath and kitchen—the rest of the house was given over to his collection in locked display cases. The spacious garage had been converted into his work area. In front of it was where his car was parked in the driveway under a canopy. A buyer or an owner had to make an appointment, with the collector doing a background check on him or her. The collector had a lot of security in and around his house.

Every cabinet was locked with the keys hidden. The ammunition was kept separate. The FBI, ATF and other alphabet agencies were focusing on those who had been in the house. Those people included his housekeeper/cook; his three assistants who helped him fix and restore the guns, a gardener and a house cleaner. One of his assistants was also the housesitter.

The housesitter lived in while the collector was at a gun show. He said the housesitter did not know where the keys or the ammunition were. And even if he found the ammunition, he wouldn't know what gun it went with.

Simone thought that belied the fact that the housesitter was also one of those who repaired and restored the guns. She thought briefly about going over to his house. Or even arranging with Jasmine to visit her brother's house next door. She wanted to but didn't. So she had to rely on Jasmine's reporting which was sporadic, as she only worked part-time. Plus she wasn't always able to talk to her brother.

Then, a little breakthrough. The brother reported the FBI had interviewed everyone who had access to the house. The theft had occurred when the owner was at a gun show, and his housesitter supposedly in residence. Neighbors had seen another man with the housesitter, but not well enough to describe him. They had seen enough to know the man wasn't anyone they had seen before. The housesitter had strict instructions not to bring anyone else into the house. On top of that, the housesitter was missing. Was he the person who supplied the shooter with the antique machine gun? He was 'a person of interest' the FBI—and others—wanted to talk with. Jasmine duly reported this over several days.

Then, one day the sun shone—she had great news—the news everyone in Simone's circle had been waiting for. Jasmine related briefly what she had learned. Simone invited her to dinner with the group, but suggested she tell the story *after* dinner. Jasmine nodded. It was a little gruesome and Jasmine had only told her in general terms.

At the long table, anticipation was high, but everyone was hungry—so eating first was fine—with Jasmine's telling as dessert of a sort.

Jasmine was a big-boned and strong woman. That helped her as a nurse. Simone discovered she was also a superb storyteller—and had a raucous laugh.

"You've got to picture the set-up," Jasmine started off. "There's an alley behind my brother's house. It runs through the middle of the block, so his house faces 4th street and the houses on the other side of the alley face 5th street. The alley is where the dumpsters are for those houses."

Jasmine paused, took a sip of wine, and Simone noticed everyone nodding their heads. Yes they could picture it.

"The guy from the house on 5th, he's back there to throw his garbage in the dumpster, but he doesn't get past his gate. He sees a woman in a police officer uniform with a dog—the German Shepherd kind. The dog heads for the dumpster, then sits down."

Another sip as Jasmine surveyed her audience.

"Then he hears a noise and so does the police officer. They look down the alley and there's the garbage truck slipping those fork things under a dumpster, lifting it up and pouring the contents into the truck. He sees the lady officer talking on her phone, looking at the truck, at the dumpster and at the dog."

The audience seemed to lean forward.

"So she whips out some of that yellow crime scene tape and starts putting it on the dumpster. The garbage truck guy comes, they have a chit-chat, he uses his phone and then drives up to the next dumpster."

"The neighbor waits, and soon the coroner's van comes along. Two guys get out, pull on those white Mars-type Haz-Mat suits and do a little dumpster diving. Only they don't have to look too far down when they come up with a large package in two blue trash bags that has black duct tape around the middle holding them together."

"Soon all of this is all over the neighborhood and I get to talk to the guy who saw it all. So I'm telling you all I know."

"Except for one thing," Simone said. She started to feel a little queasy.

"Yeah." Jasmine looked sad. She took another sip of wine. She was a nurse after all, working to save lives. "What was in the taped-together garbage bags was the body of the housesitter. No way did he commit suicide and no way was it an accidental death."

"Murder," someone at the table said.

"The shooter," someone else said.

"Did the shooter shoot him with the machine gun?" someone else asked.

Jasmine paused. Simone felt her dinner rising in her throat. Then Jasmine said, "The victim had been knocked out long enough for the shooter to wrap him up like garbage. Hands and feet tied. Hands behind him." Jasmine drained her glass. "The poor guy smothered to death."

Simone knocked over her chair in her rush to the ladies' room, stomach coming up. The cruelty of the act made her ill. As she burst through the door she ran smack into a woman coming out. The woman was vaguely familiar—Simone had seen her at the hospital. But no thought of that now. She ran to a stall and vomited a week's worth of food, it seemed like—definitely all that she had eaten at dinner.

The woman she had run into came over with damp paper towels and daubed Simone's face.

After Simone threw up all she had in her, she wiped her face with another set of damp towels, rinsed her mouth at the sink, looked in the mirror and thanked the woman. Her own reflection could have been a ghost.

"Hi, I'm Ann Simpson. You're Simone. I've come to your hospital room a couple of times but missed you. Just left a note at the motel desk for you."

Simone nodded. That's about all she could do. In a few minutes, she was able to splash water on her face and tell Ann briefly what had propelled her into the ladies room.

Ann nodded, as if she knew. "Let's get you back to your room. We can talk there, if you feel like it."

Simone nodded again and headed for the door. "I'll get my purse." The woman followed her. At the table a few asked how she was, and greeted Ann by name. They left and went to Simone's room.

Then she recognized the woman. "You did that interview with the collector. You're a reporter, I think."

"A journalist for internet service, like Reuters. We have many news agencies all over world who subscribe to our services. I was the first to be allowed to talk to him. The FBI had kept a tight lid on everything. They didn't know if it was a terrorist attack or what, and how far it extended, like to other airports. Hope it's okay if we talk. Actually, I can tell you a few more things about the body, if you want to know."

Simone gave a slight burp, but she had nothing else to bring up. She sat on the bed and gestured to Ann to sit on the only chair in the room.

"I know you've been a go-to person for the victims and their families. I'll tell you what I just learned."

Simone nodded, still feeling a little queasy. She tried not to think about the package of garbage.

"As you know the housesitter was found dead. The FBI suspects that he became friends with the shooter, or rather the shooter became friends with him. The point is the FBI suspects that it was an opportunist thing, not a planned thing. When the shooter found out what a gold mine he had in this housesitter, he mined it. The shooter stayed in the house with the housesitter for two days, at least. His DNA is there. And, of course, he was found with the missing gun at the airport, so it's sort of open and shut. But they're tying up all the loose ends. They're quite sure the housesitter had nothing to do with the plans. They've surmised that he showed off the collection and what he knew, and the shooter took advantage of that. As I said, an opportunist."

Ann grimaced, and Simone felt something in her throat. She coughed, then reached for the bottle of water on her nightstand. On second thought, maybe she'd better not have anything.

"What's interesting is that the young man had clutched in his right hand one of the rounds from the machine gun that the shooter used. The FBI thinks this was a message from the dead man. The bullet means something. It connects the housesitter to the shooter. And, of course, to the house. The collector has identified the antique machine gun as one that he was working on restoring—but not operable."

"Two bullets passed through my sister and she's on life support." Simone gulped back a sob. "I have to make the decision to pull the plug."

Ann offered her sympathy.

"Then I have to start a new life. Start over." She stood up as though she was going to start it at that moment. Ann looked startled. Simone took a deep breath and sat down again.

"All my life my sister has taken care of me. Now I'm going to pull the plug on her life. It doesn't seem to be a fair payment for all that she has done for me."

Ann started to say something, but Simone continued. "I've learned there's nothing wrong with my heart. We've always thought I had a weak heart. That's why we were going to India. My sister learned of a guru there and he was going to cure me." She gave a little laugh.

"I've been to India," Ann said, "But not the places you would see."

"Places a journalist goes?"

Ann nodded. "What do you want to do now?"

"That's the question, isn't it? After I pull the plug and follow through on the arrangements my sister has made for her…body. Mine, too, but I'm not joining her on that trip just yet."

Ann looked at her, as though still waiting for an answer.

"I'll rebook the trip to India. Is that being too selfish?"

"You're thinking like a woman. Would a man ask that question? No, he wouldn't. He would go on. He would rebook the trip to India, and he would be thankful he did. You do the same thing," Ann advised.

"I'm very angry at the shooter for interrupting our lives. I liked my life before. My sister was my best friend. I'm mad at him. I don't want to be stopped by a man with a gun. I don't want him to influence the rest of my life. I want to be able to do things, not feel afraid." Sobs choked her. "I want to go to India, show him that he can't stop me." No matter, she thought, that he's dead. He's not stopping anyone anymore. She realized her thoughts were rambling.

"Good for you. Tomorrow you'll go to the hospital, do what you have to do. And then you can rebook your flight."

Simone nodded. Would she feel as brave tomorrow, when she

saw her sister on life support and had to make the decision to end it all. See her sister breathe her last, no matter that she wasn't breathing on her own—and never would.

"Yes," Ann said, exuding confidence. "I've been to India and I envy you your trip. You will see the India as I never did. You will see it in all its glory, the Taj Mahal glittering in the sunlight. I'm told it's a sight to behold. Like the Dome of St. Peter's in Jerusalem. I've never seen that either. You have a chance to make your life different, even though you liked your old life. You now have a new one. And you have a life."

"And my sister doesn't"

"Then you have to live for her, too."

~The End~

THE GUN

Liana, a shooting victim, has a new face and wants a new life. She wants to have joie de vivre—to feel exuberance enough to want to dance in the rain. She learns more about the shooter and wonders what his life was like and why he had to shoot his parents and others at LAX. She feels sad that he, obviously, never experienced a desire to dance in the rain—but he has given her a chance to do that.

THE GUN

In the line to go through airport security, Liana was taking off her jewelry—wedding rings, necklace—when she looked up and saw a young man, maybe in his twenties, holding a stick. The older man beside her didn't see him because he was emptying his pockets into a tray. It was the younger man's face that caught her attention. Expressionless. Why was he holding out a stick? Then the end of the stick was on fire. But it wasn't fire. The man in front of her looked up and said something loudly, seemingly noticing the young man for the first time. Then he jerked a few times. Liana felt a searing pain in her left side and then her face. Suddenly she couldn't breathe.

When Liana came to, she knew she was in a hospital. The sounds and the smell. Her left side hurt, breathing was painful. Her face felt stiff, so in need of moisturizer, but she couldn't move her hands to touch it.

Two white-coated people in the room. Liana glanced around. She realized the left side of her face was bandaged, covering her eye. And she didn't have her glasses on.

"Are you having pain?"

Liana was afraid to move her head, only shifting her eye to the left to look at him. She tried to talk, but her mouth felt glued shut. She made sounds in her throat, like gargling, but that was it.

"You are going to be fine. A bullet went into your lung and another in your cheek. But we have fixed that. A little facial reconstruction. It will take a while for everything to heal. We're giving you something for your pain in the IV."

Liana turned her eye to the right and saw the line from her arm to the bag hanging from a metal support—a mini clothes tree.

Gradually she was awake more than she was asleep, sitting, then standing. Physical therapy aided her so that she was able to walk without help. Soon she could go home, they told her.

But she didn't want to go home.

Walking back to her room with the physical therapist, Liana's eye was caught by a bright blue piece of paper on the bulletin board. A rainbow arched from the bottom of the sheet to the top and back down again. Thick black letters were easy for her to see.

DANCE IN THE RAIN

Liana stopped to read it. "What does that mean?" she said out loud more to herself than to the therapist who stood next to her.

"It means you know you are better when you want to dance in the rain with *joie de vivre*—exuberant about being alive," the therapist said. "It's a mental thing."

A mental thing. *Dance in the rain* was a mental thing.

"A soft summer rain would be my choice," the therapist said.

Liana turned to her. The woman was probably twice the size she should be, wearing pink scrubs with a pattern of tiny flowers, her black curly hair snug at the back of her neck in a matching pink barrette. "Do *you* dance in the rain?"

"Don't have time. Sometimes I dance with a patient when we're exercising and she's had a breakthrough—done something she hasn't been able to do. I dance around with my kids sometimes, too. But we don't get much rain here—so I don't have a lot of opportunity to do that."

"I mean…do you have *joie de vivre*?" Liana asked, trying to understand.

"Oh, yeah. I don't think about it a lot, but yeah, I do. You will, too."

I've never had it. The thought struck her like a lightning bolt. *I've never had joie de vivre.*

Then her next thought was—*maybe that's why I don't want to go home.*

She couldn't complain about her life—at least not now with others dead and her still alive. She took a deep breath. Her heart was pounding at the memory of the shooting at the airport. She gasped at how close she'd been to dying—the realization hadn't penetrated before. Why had she been saved and others not?

113

"Are you all right?" The therapist had a frown on her forehead, her concern visible, a hand under Liana's elbow.

Liana laughed slightly, a forced laugh. "Yes, just thinking about…about what happened."

"Let's get you back to your room. Have a little rest. You did a lot of exercising today. You're coming along just fine." The woman guided her to her room. Liana settled in the chair, not the bed. "I'll get you some more water," the woman said.

"I'm fine," Liana said, suddenly seeing her life as it had been during her few disjointed talks with her husband. She couldn't talk well and he was very sick with the flu, stomach virus and whatever else was going around for him to catch.

With the bandage off her face, and her glasses on, Liana could clearly see herself in the mirror for the first time. She thought she was looking out of a window at another person. She reached up to touch the window and the woman on the other side did the same.

Liana was both women. It wasn't her face anymore.

She thought about the other 'Liana'—the pre-shooting one. That was a different person—one who had drifted through life, who had never experienced *joie de vivre*, nor any kind of exuberance. Contented, yes. Comfortable, yes. But the rainbow in her life had been colorless. Her life had been a black and white film.

It didn't have to continue that way, she could do something about it.

Liana stared at the new woman in the mirror and made a vow. No more drifting aimlessly through life. She wanted to experience *joie de vivre*, the kind that made her want to dance in the rain.

The mantle of a new persona cloaked her. She was a new person in every way. She had been given a second chance at life and now she was going to live it to the fullest.

All she had to do was find out how to do that.

She touched her brown, greying hair. That's where she'd start.

While her discharge was in process, she called her hairdresser for an appointment. "Now," Liana told her.

Once there, her hairdresser said, "I recognize the hair, but I don't recognize you."

"It's me," Liana said. "Facial reconstruction."

"I heard you were one of the victims at the airport shooting. How are you doing?"

"I'm here. Give me a completely new style and color. I want to be a different person."

"Ohhhkaaay." The hairdresser set to work. A different cut—short and feathery—and new silvery blonde hair.

Liana looked at the woman in the mirror. She smiled. The woman in the mirror smiled back.

When she unlocked the front door, Harry sprang up from his lounge chair. "Who are you?" Then he looked a little closer. "Is it really you?"

"You look different, too. You've lost weight."

"Flu and pneumonia and a few other things. But I'm okay now, not contagious. Your doctors checked with my doctors, and somebody came to look the place over, otherwise they wouldn't let you come home. I won't give you a hug, just in case."

"Kissy, kissy, back to you. I'm still a little sore so a bone-crushing hug is not on my agenda, but thanks anyway. Smiling isn't easy either."

He scrutinized her. "You don't look like my wife. How do I know it's you. You could be an imposter, trying to get my money."

"I'll get it all later. I'm going to make some tea and then I need to lie down for a while."

"You don't even sound like her. I mean your voice. The kettle broke."

"The kettle broke?" It was a ceramic electric kettle. She wasn't surprised that it broke. She didn't even care how it happened, she'd find something to boil the water in. A headache was coming on, she needed the hot tea. He followed her into the kitchen.

She pulled out a saucepan and filled it with water, and reached for the tea canister. She opened the refrigerator. No milk. In fact—nothing. And it smelled. Her headache was stronger now. She had to sit down.

All the while Harry had been watching her. "Somebody from the hospital's coming out tomorrow morning. Got it written down. Therapy."

Holding her head in her hands, she thought, *if only I could take it off like a hat, put it back on when the headache was gone.*

"Are you still sick, honey?" he asked. He moved to her side and touched her shoulder.

Yes. Sick and tired.

"It's been a busy day. This is the longest I've been up."

"I haven't got my strength back yet either."

She poured the boiling water over one teabag in the small brown pot. She made it weak because there was no milk. "I think I'll lie down on the sofa." She took the tea tray with her to the living room, sipped and drained the cup, then poured another cupful. After a few sips, she slid the cup and saucer onto the tray, then stretched out. A glance at her phone. 5:10.

Liana woke. She didn't think the light outside had changed. She turned her head slightly—good, no headache—to look at her phone on the coffee table. 5:01. That didn't make sense because she had closed her eyes at 5:10. Which meant—it was morning.

A noise. It took her a moment to recognize what it was. Harry snoring. He was on his lounge chair which was almost horizontal.

Liana thought it was sweet of him to stay with her while she slept on the sofa. Then her next thought was—that was where he had been sleeping since she left. A maroon wool alpaca throw covered him. Made sense. No sheets or pillowcase to bother with. And no pjs.

She rolled slowly off the sofa, not wanting to jiggle her head too much. She went to the kitchen to make tea. Harry had washed her teapot and cup, so they were waiting for her on the drain board. By habit she opened the refrigerator. Milk! Then she saw the newspaper folded at the crossword puzzle on the table—and a note.

Feebees want a go at you again. They will call for an apt.

Feebees? Phoebe? Liana didn't know anyone by that name. What was an apt? *Apartment?* Before she could think further she saw a box on the counter. An electric kettle! Was she dreaming—or worse— hallucinating?

Liana opened the box, read the directions, and followed the instructions. It was glass, and a blue circle of light came on around the bottom. Magical. She stood mesmerized by the color. The water boiled and the kettle clicked off. She snapped out of her trance, poured the water over the teabags in the pot, then carried the pot to the kitchen table where her cup was with milk in it. She sat and drank one cup almost in a gulp, then refilled her cup. It tasted so good. She felt her brain perking up, looking around to see where it was.

Feebees Ah! FBI. Okay.

That brought the shooting to mind. She felt twinges in her left side, and the left part of her face felt stiff. She had medical cream for it, and in time the feeling would go away, she was told.

The crossword puzzle was partially filled out by Harry—or as much as he could do. She opened the paper and read the article by Ann Simpson. She read it twice, trying to eke out more information from between the lines.

The young man had shot his parents. What had his home life been like? What had triggered the action to kill them? What had they done to provoke such a fatal act? She didn't know who was to blame— the parents or their child. Had his growing up been so terrible?

She felt a pang of sorrow for him. He had never experienced *joie de vivre*, had never been exuberant enough to dance in the rain.

What more could she tell the FBI pair other than what she'd said at the hospital? She had been fairly compos mentis. The FBI team—a man and woman—had interviewed all of the victims. Liana didn't know how many. Five had died outright at the airport. She wasn't sure what the body count was now. She had asked, but the answer had been vague.

Maybe they were still counting. Maybe those who made it to the hospital didn't make it out. She was sure she wasn't the only one who survived. She had been one of the ones more seriously wounded, she knew that.

Her distinction, if it could be so named, was that she had seen the face of the shooter closer than others had. At least, those who were still alive. "But isn't he dead? What difference does it make now?" she had asked of the FBI team.

The woman had answered. "We want to be sure he didn't have any accomplices. That he was the only one shooting. We have to be sure that the dead man was the shooter and that no one else placed the gun in his hands."

That seemed a little far-fetched, but Liana wasn't an FBI Agent.

What she thought about was his face. Like a death mask. Like a face that had had too many facelifts and was immobile. Completely smooth. He was young, but somehow that didn't seem real. It was the facelifts that gave the impression of a young man. She tried to tell them this, describe what her impression was, but she couldn't seem to do it to her satisfaction. The bottom line was the only way she could describe his face was impassive as though made of *papier mache*—no expression of determination, or hatred, or whatever a face would show when shooting several people with a machine gun. He could have been watering the lawn as easily as spraying people with bullets. His eyes were as dead as the people.

The snoring in the living room became a couple of loud snorts. A few minutes later Harry appeared in the doorway. "Did you make coffee?" he said teasingly.

"You're welcome to a cup of tea." She knew he'd never drink that. "Water's still hot, have some Nescafe." Liana's stomach did a flip-flop at the thought. "Think I'll take a shower."

"Some lady's coming at 9 to be sure you are still alive."

"Yeah, think I am still alive. Maybe more than I was before the shooting. Actually feel pretty good. Physical therapy and social worker are the ones coming. Thanks for the kettle," she said.

"Had it in the car. Forgot to bring it in. Sick, you know. Working okay?"

She nodded. "And thanks for the milk."

"I'm real glad you're home, honey. Now we can get back to normal."

Liana gasped. *Normal. No, no, not normal.*

After drinking her tea, Liana made her way to the stairs, grasping the bannister and pulling herself up the stairs with her right hand. Their bedroom was at the top of the stairs, like a large enclosed sunporch, windows on three sides. She pulled off all her clothes, letting them drop, one by one, to the floor. She checked her phone. 7:14.

The deliciousness of a shower. Her own shampoo of orange blossoms. Jasmine soap. No heavy smell of disinfectant. Ah, heaven.

Now—what to wear. She stood in front of the open doors of the wardrobe—it was a big old-fashioned one of heavy dark wood. What did she feel like—something with color. A red hibiscus-patterned silk shirt and red long pants. That made a statement in her new life. In her old life she never would have put them together. She sighed with relief that she was starting her new life.

New life day. Liana sat on a white wicker chair at the matching table in the corner of the bedroom, still smelling the scent of the orange and jasmine wafting on dissipating steam vapors from the bathroom just a few feet away.

She had a small notepad open on the table and held a fine-tipped pen, her laptop open First, she was going to write down all the things she liked to do.

Opera performances—usher

Plays—backstage work

Reading. Working with books. Library. Bookstore

Archaeology—a dig in Egypt

Traveling—agent, tour leader

Liana thought about her A.A. from the local community college. She hadn't majored in anything, so was allowed to take five extra elective courses. She took stage management, broadcasting, landscape architecture, first aid, and—butterflies.

That's it! That's what she would do. She'd go back and get her B.A. She stopped. In what? Look online and see what the university offered. Wait. Her new life. Did she want to move to another state to attend school? First, she should decide what she wanted to major in and then go to the best school for that. If she stayed home would she have a new life?

"You must be feeling better." Harry stood in the doorway.

"I am. I've decided to go back to school, get my B.A."

"You're definitely better then if you're thinking that. Just wanted to remind you about your appointment. It's almost 9, time for one of those ladies to appear."

"Send up whoever comes."

Harry nodded.

She went online to look at the nearby university's catalog. She scrolled through the list of degree subjects offered. She felt excitement in the process, not focusing on anything in particular, just looking at them all. A few made her heart skip a beat. Then there it was.

Tourism, Hospitality and Recreation Management

Liana read the words three times then clicked on the *Program Requirements*. Her heart raced. *Practicum and interning*—perfect. And the electives were amazing. She could choose from Backpacking, Rock Climbing, Winter Mountaineering, Flat- and White-water Boating, Survival, Challenge / Rope Courses, Caving, Waterskiing, Sailing. And those were just the outdoor ones. Could she sign up for all of them?

She registered online under her middle and birth name, dropping her first name. All three had been on her A.A. certificate. A new persona for a new life!

Should she thank the shooter? She couldn't get that image of those dead eyes and face devoid of any expression out of her mind. Dead eyes in a dead face.

The man beside her at the airport, the one who had been emptying his pockets, was the father of the shooter. Why did the son go to the airport to kill them? He must have had other opportunities. And the machine gun, antique at that, stolen from a collector. Why that gun?

He must have known that he would be killed by standing in the middle of the airport terminal shooting at people. He was. Officers from different agencies had shot bullets into him.

Should she go online and soak up all of the news of the shooting? She didn't want to relive it. Every time she thought about it, her side and cheek hurt. Then she had to gasp for breath, which only hurt more. She was done with it. Let the dead bury their own dead.

Liana sat back. She was getting what she wanted—a new life. The pursuit of happiness, of *joie de vivre*—that's the path she was on.

She was going to dance in the rain.

~The End~